VET IN POWER

Despite the outrageous circumstances which bring Briony Beaumont to work for fellow veterinary surgeon Nick Lloyd, she is determined to make the best of it — and even she has to admit that Nick's surgery is impressive. But nothing else is certain with Nick . . . Briony is sure he is playing cat-and-mouse games with her emotions — so why can't she stop herself reacting to him?

CAROL WOOD

VET IN POWER

Complete and Unabridged

LINFORD
Leicester

First published in Great Britain in 1993

First Linford Edition
published 2013

A catalogue record for this book is available
from the British Library.

ISBN 978–1–4448–1651–8

Published by
F. A. Thorpe (Publishing)
Anstey, Leicestershire

Set by Words & Graphics Ltd.
Anstey, Leicestershire
Printed and bound in Great Britain by
T. J. International Ltd., Padstow, Cornwall

This book is printed on acid-free paper

1

'I would give anything, Briony, not to have to bother you with my problems . . . but I just don't know who else to turn to.'

Briony Beaumont, as tall as her ex-jockey brother at five feet nine and as like him as two peas in a pod, with their unruly manes of dark coppery hair, felt the familiar ache of sympathy run through her.

'Don, take things easy,' she persuaded gently, peeling off her windcheater as they walked into the kitchen from the stable-yard. Falling into a chair, she gazed around. 'Oh, Don, this room is beautiful. You and Beth have done wonders!'

'I suppose so.' He poured coffee from the percolator into large china mugs. 'Sorry to have to bring you all the way down from the Dales . . . I put off phoning for as long as I could.'

Don Beaumont, lithe and slim in his thirtieth year, walked across the kitchen, an imperceptible limp tugging at his left leg. Handing her a mug, he said, 'Thanks for coming, Sis.'

She smiled up at him. Had he lost weight? She took a sip and felt the refreshing liquid slide warmly down, noting too the drawn skin over his cheekbones. Trying not to let her concern show, she gazed around the kitchen. New units in pine, lavish working-tops, and a brilliant new cooking range which looked more like something out of *Star Wars*. 'I still can't get over this place. The house was virtually derelict when I came a couple of years back.'

'We spent far more on renovation than we planned. Still another stable-block to be done too. Heaven only knows, a three-mile steeplechase in pouring rain with a nag in blinkers isn't as bad a prospect as all this.'

So was that the trouble? Was he still pining for his old flame, racing? He must have realised by now that the accident in his last race had put paid to his career. But she thought he'd got over all that. The stables, surely, were doing well?

'Can you stay for a bit?' he asked, coming to sit by her.

'I'd love to, if Beth doesn't mind.'

Although Don's urgent telephone call had brought Briony in a hurry from Yorkshire, coincidentally it had come during the last week of her job working for a small veterinary practice. Five years away from the part of England in which she had grown up had only deepened her longing to be back home, though until recently she hadn't admitted the fact even to herself. Today, passing through the velvet Downs that rolled like a quilted sea from Salisbury, she felt her heart leap at its familiar beauty.

'To be honest with you, Don, your call isn't the only reason I'm here. You see, I gave in my notice to Greg a month ago. Yesterday was my last day.'

'But I thought you were in Yorkshire for good?'

She had hardly imagined her decision was going to be so difficult to explain! 'I was . . . yes. I'd even tentatively picked out a practice to build up. But when it came to it I suppose I just got cold feet.'

'You're not going back to Father, to Amberfields?' Don's forehead creased in a frown.

'No, silly!' How could her brother even suggest going home? They'd both had struggles enough to assert their independence in their teens — Amberfields was hardly an alternative now! 'When I left home, I left for good . . . and with Mum gone it just wouldn't be the same anyway.'

'So you'll find a practice locally?'

'Yes, why not?'

'Then you must stay while you look around. The bedrooms are all done now, most of the house is finished except for the roof. We still have a few leaks here and there, but you'll be quite comfortable.'

4

'If you're sure ... ' Briony took another gulp of coffee, sensing trouble. Perhaps she ought not to impose. A temporary flat might be a better idea.

Through the lattice windows she noticed the lads busily preparing for evening stables. At this hour Don would normally be out there on his rounds supervising the last few jobs. Strange ... ? She eased her long, slim legs, clad in oatmeal ski-pants, to full stretch, observing her brother through lowered lids. 'Mm ... it's just like old times.' Closing her eyes, she breathed in the leathery smell of the house, a fragrance she always connected with home. When she opened them, Don was staring at her. She gave him a nervous laugh, seeing the tension in his face. 'Come on, then, out with it, big brother. What's up?'

He shook his head slowly. 'Just about everything, really. Cash flow, for a start. I've a massive bill to be settled at the feed merchant. With thirty horses out there champing their way through feed it's not surprising either.'

'Aren't the owners paying their fees on time?'

'The season's been poor; naturally they don't want to fork out. But October, November, December . . . they're usually good months for us if we can sit tight. To raise some money I've decided to sell Phoebe, my brood mare. When she's foaled, I'll look around for a buyer. She comes from excellent stock, so I shouldn't have any trouble.'

'Phoebe? You've had her for a long while, haven't you? Surely you won't want to sell her?'

He shrugged. 'I've no choice. I have to find some capital somewhere.'

'Is the feed merchant the only bill that's worrying you?'

Don dismally shook his head again. 'No, I'm afraid not. There's the blacksmith, the transport people and . . . the vet.'

Briony almost choked on her coffee. 'The vet? But you can't not pay your vet!'

'I know it, Briony, but I can't pay anyone at the moment!'

'But you must have something?'

She saw the sideways look he gave her and her tummy turned. 'I did a silly thing, you see,' he told her, his voice weak. 'There was this horse, John Jimini . . . I put all our spare cash on him to win to get us out of this scrape.'

'But I thought you didn't bet any more . . . ' Hadn't he kicked the habit? She'd assumed it was just a replacement high for racing, thinking the urge would pass when he became more established in his business of training thoroughbreds. She hadn't realised it had got such a hold.

'I don't bet. It was just a spur-of-the-moment decision. Alan Dale, the jockey, was convinced he was on form.'

'He lost, I suppose?'

Don nodded miserably.

'You promised Beth you'd never bet again. What in heaven's name did she say?'

He lowered his eyes, unable to meet

her stare. 'Beth has left me. Oh, Briony, what am I going to do? The house, the stables — they don't mean a thing without her.'

Briony watched, hardly knowing what to say. She felt sorry for her brother, but it wasn't as if he'd been gagged and blindfolded into losing money so foolishly! And Beth had been so loyal to him over the years, sticking by him through thick and thin.

Don had dated her when he first left home to become a professional jockey. When the accident happened two years later, a bad fall over a fence, Briony remembered it was Beth who had encouraged him to go it alone with his own business. Being the fiercely intelligent young woman she was, she'd known that if Don was persuaded back into his father's training stables at Amberfields Ralph's dominance would crush him eventually.

'Come on,' she said gently. 'Beth will be back. You've had far worse times. Do you remember Father's face when I told him I was going to be a vet? You'd come home to introduce Beth to the family and found yourself in the middle of World War Three. What a weekend!'

She was relieved when a smile edged his lips. 'I'll never forget it! Thank God Mum was able to arrange for you to go and live with Aunt Grace in Yorkshire. I doubt that we'd have won any more battles with him.'

Briony's mind slipped back to the long journey north and the beginning of her life in the Dales with Aunt Grace. Her mother's sister had even arranged for her to continue her studies despite her father's opposition. Ralph Beaumont had been furious. But his anger had turned to anguish when her mother, Sophie, died prematurely from a heart condition. Ironically Briony's results had come through, seven days too late.

Soon after, Greg Harding had offered her a post in his busy one-man practice. He and his wife had been more like adoptive parents. And when, six months later, Aunt Grace passed away, they had encouraged her to think of the future instead of brooding, to think of what she really wanted to do with her life. And so, with the small nest-egg she had saved, she had begun to formulate plans in her mind for her own practice . . .

Don was looking downcast again. That was his trouble. Without Beth to inject life into him he could easily sink back into depression. 'Have you chivvied up your owners to pay their bills?' she asked, watching him carefully.

'No. I wouldn't let Beth do it. She wanted to ask outright for our money.'

'You should have. You've trained their horses, now they have to pay you.'

'I know I failed her . . . ' For a moment, as Don dragged a hand through his thick, wiry hair, she had the dreadful feeling he was going to break down. But something outside in the yard distracted him. Rushing in stockinged feet to see what was going on, he reached the window. 'It's Phoebe. She's acting up!'

Briony hurried beside him, pressing her nose against the window. 'Does she often behave like that?'

'She's a bit temperamental lately — pregnancy, I suppose. What the hell are those lads doing? She'll catch her leg in the reins if someone doesn't stop her.'

He disappeared, cursing his boots.

No one seemed to have the least bit of control over Phoebe, for all the shouting and yelling that was going on. It horrified Briony to think of what might happen if she did entrap her legs.

Seconds later she found herself in the yard, the cold air stinging her cheeks. Panic had set in and the other horses had sensed it. 'Get those horses back into their boxes!' she yelled at the stable lads. The young assistants turned to see a female replica of Don Beaumont, a cloud of coppery hair swirling about her shoulders, and each one of them scattered to do her bidding without waiting to be told twice.

'You over there!' Briony called to a figure near Phoebe. 'Don't just stand there . . . grab her reins!'

Crazily, the figure hesitated — and almost fell under Phoebe's hoofs. A shout of warning rose in her throat as her long legs carried her towards the man who was obviously half-asleep! Rugby tackles weren't her speciality, but in a case like this . . .

The collision knocked all the breath from her body — and probably from his too. But at least they were down on the ground. The slashing of air above them made her keep very still, spread-eagled with her arms protecting her face. If Don didn't get to her before those hoofs came down in the small of her back . . .

A groan suddenly came from below her and she felt the pounding of the man's heart against her own. At least he was alive. She'd seen the pallor of his face as she'd landed on him, and in that instant she'd known there was something dreadfully wrong.

'Stay where you are, Bri!' Her brother's voice was close now. 'Don't move, for goodness' sake, I've almost got her.' Hoping Don's horsemanship was more skilful than his business acumen, she didn't move an inch.

'Damn! Let me get up!' A gritty voice bit into the tangled skeins of her hair and a pair of arms wrapped around her. She blinked uncertainly, lifting herself a fraction. Then she saw the gash. Across his forehead, blood and jutting skin mingled in an ugly wound.

'You're going to be all right . . . but just lie still for a moment.' She could hardly believe her own optimism. That was a nasty wound, one a lot of people would be out cold with. She flattened her palms on his chest in an effort to prevent him from moving. He was a big man, broad-shouldered, with a muscular chest that felt hot under her hands. Oddly she had a faint feeling she had seen him before, and her heart suddenly raced.

'What the devil's going on?'
The darkest eyes she had ever seen looked back at her. Maybe they were

black, perhaps a very dark brown, and the pupils looked hazy, just as though he was about to pass out. Phoebe must have inflicted the damage before Briony and Don had rushed from the house — probably he had been only semi-conscious when she had floored him!

'I told Beaumont I wanted to sedate her — I told him!' The eyes, the voice, the thin scar running along the lower jawbone — somehow they all seemed familiar . . . it couldn't possibly be . . . no, she must be imagining things!

'It isn't . . . Nick Lloyd?' she gasped, her eyes as wide as saucers.

He appeared to recognise her in the same instant. As he mouthed her name with equal astonishment, she watched an energy fill the face, as though life was flooding back into him. 'You sent me flying,' he grumbled hotly in the next instant.

'I had to, I'm afraid. You're injured. There's a wound on your forehead.'

'Do you mind if we get up now?'

'Yes . . . of course. Here, let me help you.' Scrambling to her feet, Briony put out her hand to help him up, but he shook his head and stood up, swaying slightly on his feet.

'I'm all right. Stop fussing, for heaven's sake.'

'I was only trying to help you.'

'Help would have been useful half an hour ago when there was no one about!' A large weathered hand came up to push back the mop of thick ebony hair flecked at the temples with grey. 'I was in the process of using a gag and twitch to rasp that blessed mare's mouth, when she decided she wasn't going to have any of it. If I'd had my way in the first place I'd have sedated her.'

Briony's mouth fell open. 'You're Don's vet?'

Nick Lloyd was the last person she had expected to find in her brother's yard . . . though now she thought about it, hadn't both Nick and Luke Lloyd taken degrees in medicine? She'd

15

known the family from ever since she could remember. They had been immediate neighbours, their lands adjacent to Amberfields. Like Ralph Beaumont, Sebastian Lloyd was a trainer, and there had been rivalry between them for years. She'd heard that Nick and Luke had left home and that afterwards Sebastian had sold up his estates and stables. She'd assumed Bagbourne would be the last place on earth she would ever see Nick again.

'I thought you'd left the area,' she said blankly. 'I didn't expect to find you here of all places.'

'Who else but a vet would have their head inside a horse's mouth?' he muttered under his breath.

She peered at him warily, wondering if he was suffering from concussion. 'You were probably right about sedating Phoebe,' she said, hoping this might placate him, but seeing at once that it didn't.

Glaring at her, he demanded, 'And how would you know, may I ask?'

'Well . . . you see . . . I'm a vet too, actually.'

The dark eyes widened in disbelief. 'You're joking! A little thing like you . . . why, you were no more than a kid when I last saw you.'

'Exactly sixteen,' provided Briony, wishing at once that she'd kept quiet. Having a raging crush on Nick Lloyd had been the most painful and delicious phenomenon of her teens. She would have died rather than admit it, though she suspected he might have got an inkling, falling over a rather gauche and gangling fifteen-year-old everywhere he went. But surely it was too long ago for him to remember?

Glimmering white teeth flashed momentarily, showing her he had not forgotten either. 'Wasn't it Bagbourne's Young Rider Cup? How could I possibly forget? You fell off your mount at the last fence — isn't that right? — after completing the course the wrong way around, if my memory serves me correctly.'

17

It was obvious his memory served him very well. She cringed at the thought of the day she'd ridden out with a new pony, showing off under the noses of everyone, including Nick and his brother. Stupidly she'd allowed her mount to follow its nose — which happened to be to the refreshments kiosk! The last straw had come when she'd been thrown, ignominiously, at Nick's feet. He'd rushed to help her up, of course, and that had been the very worst part — the humiliation of looking into those dark eyes and not being able to produce a coherent thank-you.

But this was ridiculous!

She was almost twenty-six now, not a starry-eyed teenager any longer. Apart from which she ought to be cleaning that wound rather than standing here ogling him!

'Er — come into the house. I'll phone for a doctor and meanwhile bathe your forehead, see how deep the cut is.'

'No, thank you.' He moved in the

opposite direction. 'I'll drive myself in to Casualty.'

'But you can't! Not like that. At least wait until Don comes. He'll drive you.'

'I don't need anyone's help. I can manage.' His profile bore the hard clarity of someone who had made up his mind and was not going to be persuaded otherwise.

Luckily Don arrived, running breathlessly across the yard. 'Are you two all right . . . ? Oh, my God, Nick, that's a hell of a cut you've got there.'

'Don't ever again try and talk me out of what I know I should do!' Nick growled at Don and, hunching his shoulders, he strode off.

Briony stared at her brother in disbelief. 'Why in heaven's name didn't you tell me Nick was your vet?'

'Give me a break, Bri — I've hardly had time! I was going to. As a matter of fact I thought you'd be pleased about it, seeing that it sort of puts paid to the friction of the past between the two families.'

Briony sighed impatiently. 'Well, of course I'm pleased! That's not the point, Don. I just felt a bit of an idiot not knowing, thinking he was a groom or a stable-hand or something.'

'Sorry, Sis . . . actually he's been damned decent about the money I owe him — '

'Oh, no! I'd forgotten that. You mean it's Nick Lloyd you're in debt to?'

Don reddened guiltily. 'Now don't fly off the handle. I know what you're going to say — that the family has some pride to uphold and a Lloyd is the last person I should be owing money to. Well, I know you're right . . . but the fact is I've got myself in a mess, and somehow I'm going to have to find a way out of it.'

She sighed, giving up. 'You mean we are going to have to find a way out of it — '

'Just a moment — where does he think he's going?' Don cut in, peering after Nick.

'He says he's going to drive to

Casualty. I tried to stop him, but he's as stubborn as a mule. Can't you make him see sense?'

'He won't take kindly to me lecturing him,' Don frowned. 'Besides, Phoebe's in a terrible state. I ought to go back to her.'

'So that leaves muggins here, I suppose?'

He beamed her a radiant smile. 'That's my girl! Lavish some charm on him and he'll be putty in your hands. And — er — while you're at it, do you think you could possibly persuade him into giving me a breathing space . . . moneywise, I mean?'

* * *

Fifteen minutes later Briony was at the wheel of her convertible sports car, wondering just how she had managed to get herself into such a predicament.

Putty in her hands, Don had said.

More like concrete. As tough and hard as!

At least she'd managed to talk him into letting her drive him to hospital, though he had protested up until the moment she began to describe a pile-up on the motorway caused by a black-out!

Naturally, she could understand his attitude. After all, he'd nearly been kicked senseless.

'How are you feeling?' She gave him a sly glance.

'Not bad . . . considering.'

'I'm really sorry about Phoebe's behaviour.'

'You needn't try buttering me up. That horse was temperamental from the start. Typical! I should never have got involved with the Beaumonts again.'

Briony kept her eyes calmly on the road. 'Do I take it you're still harbouring grudges from the past? I thought it was only our fathers who resorted to childish quarrelling.'

He glared at her. 'I don't give a damn about the past! But when I have a couple of inches of flesh ripped out of

22

my forehead, I'm apt to be a little short on pleasantries. Now let's leave the subject alone and try to get some mileage out of this tin can.'

Tin can, was it? If it weren't for this tin can, Briony thought crossly, he would probably have wound up in a heap beside the road. But his words had struck home, and every time he dabbed blood from his head she felt shivers run through her.

'There are some tissues in the glove pocket.'

'Thank you, but no, thank you.' He persisted in dabbing with his clean handkerchief.

She felt very bad about the pain he was in, though he didn't complain. In fact he tried not to let her see just how much blood there was escaping from the wound. She would have liked to stop the car for a moment and check it, but no doubt that would only make him worse. Instead she put her foot down, clenching the wheel grimly, hoping he didn't lose consciousness —

or his temper — before she got to the hospital.

'I didn't say grow wings,' he muttered as they arrived at Casualty with a screech of brakes. Easing his legs from the low seat, he began to get out.

'Wait!' Briony cried, to no avail. Scrambling out, she called over the roof of the car, 'Nick, wait, I'll come with you!'

Fleetingly he turned back as he got to the big double doors. 'Don't wait around,' she heard on the wind. 'I'll manage.'

She drove twice around the hospital, then decided to park. Her conscience was pricking . . . and Nick did seem rather like a huge wounded bear whose growl was worse than his bite. The least she could do was to wait and see if his temper improved after he had seen a doctor.

The enquiry desk was busy, but finally Briony got to the receptionist. 'I'm looking for a tall gentleman with an injury to the forehead. He came in about ten minutes ago.'

The receptionist eyed her. 'Mr Lloyd, you mean. He's with Dr Westerley at the moment. He said a friend would probably be along and could give details. You were there when the accident happened, I gather?'

Briony nodded, feeling doubly guilty. 'Yes, I was, but you see — '

'Just a brief outline, then, please.'

She found herself providing one — the matter of the sedation, the rasping and the rugby tackle. The receptionist closed her book, then without smiling turned her attention to the next casualty.

Briony sighed, wishing she felt less like a criminal. She had noticed, though, a small light at the end of the tunnel. Nick had actually calculated that she would wait. She smiled to herself as she strolled into the corridor. He was a strange kettle of fish.

After a while, two student nurses passed by, engrossed in conversation. Much too restless to sit down, she followed them along the corridor.

'Who is he? He's gorgeous! I've never seen such a chest . . . and those eyes . . . they seemed to look right through me!'

Briony sheltered behind a large cheese plant, her ears pricking as the nurses stopped to peer into a cubicle.

'I took him through to X-Ray. That mat of hair . . . did you see it? Dark like a forest, over all that deliciously brown skin.'

Briony peered through the green leaves. Out from a cubicle strode Nick — fully clothed. Mildly disappointed that he was, she squinted up her eyes, listening.

'The X-rays are fine,' the young doctor was saying, 'but you should really let us keep you in, Nick, just for obs — you know the routine well enough.'

Nick shook his head, hair now slicked back into place with a formidable-looking wad of gauze protecting the wound. Even while he was listening to the doctor he gave Briony the impression of restless energy, impatient to be on the move. For a man who had taken the full force of Phoebe's frustration he was incredible!

'Be careful for a few days — and phone for someone to drop you off tonight,' Dr Westerley advised as he said goodbye to Nick.

Briony moved out from her viewpoint, walking slowly towards him. 'That looks much better!' Her eyes changed course and ran down to the tiny whorls of black hair poking out from under the shirt. His collar lay open, giving her a direct view of the smooth brown skin. 'I — er — take it you had to have stitches?' she asked, wrenching her eyes back to his face.

A pair of black eyebrows jerked together, not an altogether pleasant phenomenon. 'I did. Fortunately a friend of mine was on duty, Anderley Westerley. He rushed me through, otherwise I don't think I'd have bothered waiting.'

'You wouldn't? You're not serious, surely?' She couldn't believe he would be so impatient or so reckless.

'No lectures, thank you. Are you going to give me a lift?'

'Well, yes . . . naturally. I've got the car parked right outside.'

'This is your good deed for the day, is it?' he muttered sardonically as they walked through Casualty. 'Or is it more like guilt feelings for what happened at your brother's place?'

Briony bit her bottom lip, reminding herself that this was a man who had a headache, coming under the category of extenuating circumstances. She said cautiously, 'It's probably a little of both, to be honest.'

Nick seemed to study her for a long while as if trying to make up his mind. Then, with a reluctant grin as they pushed through the swing doors, he said in an amused voice, 'I'll need a tin-opener to get me out of that box of yours once I'm in. Couldn't you find anything more suitable to drive?'

'It's reliable, and I've had it for years. I like old, cosy, comfortable things.'

He peered at her doubtfully, raising an eyebrow. 'Where are you parked? We've got a three-mile walk, I suppose?'

She grinned as they stepped out into the fresh air. 'There are wheelchairs provided for the use of patients, but I didn't think you'd take very kindly to my suggesting one.'

'If I can hardly get in your car I doubt very much whether I'd be able to cram into one of those things. And even if I did you'd never get me out.'

She giggled, liking the dry humour when it surfaced. Something in his face reminded her, with a little stab of pain and pleasure, just how it was years ago, when the temerity of youth had driven her to desperate measures, like waiting hours outside a cinema into which she had seen him go with a girlfriend, just to get a look at him again as he emerged.

They arrived safely and she unlocked the passenger door. 'It is rather a long way down there,' she mumbled apologetically, looking at her low seat. 'Do you think you'll make it?'

His lips twisted in a wry smile. 'I'm not geriatric — yet.'

Once they were started he gave her directions, which, she noted, were to his surgery and not to his home. Suddenly remembering Don, she decided now was as good a time as any to ask for the favour. Nick could only bite her head off again! She took a deep breath, keeping her eyes on the road. 'Don will pay you back . . . at least, he won't be able to do it right away. In fact, he's decided to sell his best brood mare, Phoebe . . . but it will take time . . . rather longer than he anticipated.'

Her uncomfortable passenger tried to stretch his legs and failed. 'Time, is it now? How long does he want? A year, three years, a lifetime? I'm a vet, doesn't he realise — not the Bank of England?'

Briony changed down a gear and fell into silence.

Nick drummed his fingers on a cramped knee and clicked his tongue, looking around her car as though he would like to reconstruct it, panel by panel. Five minutes passed by without a word and then he said, 'Just here . . . turn right into the tarmac drive and the car park.'

She did as she was told. Wondering what Don would say when she arrived home and told him speaking to Nick had been like talking to a brick wall, she barely noticed her passenger extricate himself from the car with a groan.

The next thing she knew he was looking into her window, all six feet two of him bending down, the white patch glinting like a third eye. She wound down the window, smiling in spite of it.

'Well . . . goodnight . . . ' she began, her words getting stuck in her throat as a large hand held on to her door.

'You'd better come in and have a look around.' There it was, no real invitation, more a direct command.

Swallowing, she shook her head. 'It really isn't necessary. I don't want to put you out.'

'If you were putting me out,' he said, cupping her elbow with his hand and firmly easing her out of her seat, 'I wouldn't be asking you, now would I?'

2

Briony was desperate to get home, to soak in a hot bath and spoil herself. And to make things worse, as they walked together up the long drive, she found herself imagining Don pacing the floor.

'You haven't surgery, have you?' she asked as a last-ditch attempt to delay going in.

The hand was still attached to her elbow. 'We've no surgery this evening — though there should be. I'm short-staffed. My partner is in the States and I haven't been able to get anyone to replace him.'

The drive led on towards a long, low building built on a split level.

'How long is he away for?'

'Jack's committed to staying out there until he compiles enough research for the work we're doing together.' She felt Nick's scrutiny as he quickly changed the subject. 'Weren't you living in the north with a relative, something like that?'

'My mother's sister, actually, Aunt Grace.' She found herself telling him about her work in the Dales with Greg and her infrequent visits home after her mother died. She realised she'd managed to cover five years very well in the five minutes' walk to the surgery.

'And you're back for good?' he asked when she finally ran out of breath.

'For the foreseeable future, yes. I'd like to specialise in companion animals. I've done rather a lot of large animal work; I'd rather like a change now.'

'Some practices need more stamina than others,' he agreed, stopping at the double-fronted glass doors. 'I expect it toughened you up.'

'It did,' she agreed, a little put out with his lack of sympathy.

He appeared to be fishing in his pocket for keys. He mumbled, 'So why come back here? You sound as if you had those people in the palm of your hand. You'd easily have got a practice going.'

She shrugged, hoping he would hurry up and find the keys. She was beginning to shiver in her thin wind-cheater. The sooner this was over the better, and she could get back to Don. 'I missed home . . . not Amberfields particularly, but home to this part of the country. Most people have to make a decision about their roots some time in their life . . . '

The keys found, Nick inserted them and swung open the door. She asked, curious now, 'What happened after I last saw you? You got your degree, that was the last I heard.'

He ushered her into the warmth. 'Oh . . . I travelled a bit. My mother died while I was away, unfortunately. Then my father sold up and went to Scotland. I'd always planned on having a practice in the Salisbury area specialising with horses. It was when I met Jack again after being at university together that we decided to set up the group . . . ' He stopped, his eyes narrowing, tiny lines springing out from the corners. 'But I shan't bore you with the details — much as I'm tempted to. Well, what do you think of the place?'

Briony gazed around. It looked more like the foyer of the Savoy than a veterinary surgery. Soft reclining chairs and glossy magazines graced a careful colour scheme, pastels and spilling green plants with tranquil prints on the walls.

'Like it?'

She nodded, taking in her breath.

'Come along, I'll show you the ground floor.'

She wondered why on earth she wasn't making some excuse to get away, but her curiosity, as usual, had got the better of her. 'You're on twenty-four-hour call, of course?' she asked, following the broad shoulders.

'We have an arrangement with another local vet if none of us is available. The demand for twenty-four-hour attention has escalated to such an extent that we have at least two resident nurses on site.'

'And I thought Greg's practice was hectic!'

He turned back, an amused look in his eye. 'It's all relative, isn't it? The more you expand, the greater the need. Though I'm not sure which comes first. This is Reception.'

Reception turned out to be a vast, flower-filled room sprinkled with magazines and benches, altogether unlike the cramped spaces Briony had been used to working in. Greg would have drooled, she thought, if he could have seen it.

'It's beautiful! How long have you been established?'

'Four years. Do you remember Charles Wilkinson . . . Bagbourne's one and only ancient vet? He retired and I took over the original site in town.' The eyes, slightly hooded now, shading the chocolate irises, fixed her, making her feel suddenly nervous. They seemed to generate the most peculiar sensation in the pit of her stomach. Nick moved back out into the hall and beckoned her to follow. 'When we came a Portakabin served as our surgery until this was built. Jack Downey joined me, and things took off. I'd hoped Luke might come in on the business — he qualified as a toxicologist . . . but he decided to emigrate.'

'So there are only the two of you, Jack and yourself?'

'No, four in all. There's Lea Hughes. She's had eighteen months' experience with us and is our small animal vet. Then I've got a newly qualified graduate, Ben Hall, doing farm work with me — and there are two nurses, Lorraine and Anita. They live in the flat above the surgery. Incidentally, how much experience have you had in Yorkshire?'

'Three years . . . ' Realising they had come to the end of the hall and another long corridor led off to the right and another to the left with stairs running up out of one, Briony stopped, bewildered.

'A little confusing at first, isn't it? Those are the theatres and prep to the left, consulting-rooms to the right.' It was obvious he was proud of his achievements. Perhaps the guided tour was simply due to male ego, the power drive. And in a way she couldn't help but admire him.

'Have you no ... commitments? Never thought of marriage?' he asked suddenly, making her start. This was becoming more like an interrogation. What was he driving at, and why did he want to know so much about her? But his face was a blank, as though he was just being polite and showing her some interest.

Cautiously she answered, 'Well, yes, naturally I've thought of it — what woman doesn't? But thinking is as far as I've got. I want a practice of my own first — and if I've time for a relationship later on — '

'A relationship?' The dark eyes glittered. 'That sounds very clinical. Are you one of the new liberated breed, then?'

Was he talking about dogs or horses, for goodness' sake?

He drew his lower lip in fractionally before releasing it, raising the thick black eyebrows. 'You look surprised I should ask that. Don't most career women fall into that category these days? After all, ambition changes a person. It drives them to lengths they may not normally take, changes character even. Professional women, I would say, are no less ambitious than their male counterparts.'

'Supposing you're right,' she conceded sharply, 'is there something wrong with that?'

He paused. 'Not as long as ambition is recognised for what it is — and a man isn't duped into thinking he's found a fragile little nest-maker, only to discover later he's sharing his life with a bird of prey.'

She gaped at him. 'That's a terribly cynical way of looking at it!'

'But realistic.'

'I'm afraid I can't agree with you.' She watched the strikingly handsome face tighten as he made an obvious effort not to prolong the disagreement. But surely he didn't imagine all women who sought out a career were like that? Of course she wanted to fall in love, to be married, to have a family. She was old-fashioned enough to believe they were the ingredients which made a woman's life complete! Why she had used the word relationship she didn't know. Probably because he made her nervous, as he was doing right now with that penetratingly dark stare of his.

'Nick? Is everything all right? Oh, I'm sorry . . . I didn't realise you had company.' A young woman dressed in a white coat with short dark hair fashionably bobbed descended the flight of stairs behind them.

'Hello, Lea.' Nick moved to greet her. 'Sorry to disturb you . . . I should have phoned.' He made a formal introduction, during which time Briony felt the sparkling violet eyes cover her from head to toe.

'Nick, whatever's happened to your head?' A dainty hand went up to touch the bruised skin just beneath the wound.

'Nothing to worry about. My own stupid fault.'

Briony watched, interested to note the other woman's overt body language, receiving the clear message she was spelling out in defence of her property.

'You'll have to excuse us, Lea,' Nick said briskly as the feminine hand slipped back to a neat white pocket. 'I'm going to be here for a while, so if you want to shoot off, go ahead.'

'Fine . . . ' The lips, perfectly coated in plum red, smiled vaguely in Briony's direction, but the voice was distinctly frosty. 'Perhaps I'll see you again, Miss Beaumont?'

Intrigued by the undercurrents, Briony smiled, watching the shapely calves float back up the staircase.

'Our accommodation for resident staff is on the first floor, though Lea has a flat of her own in town,' Nick explained, oblivious apparently to what had just transpired. 'This is Jack's room.' He pushed open another door. 'It's unused at the moment.'

Briony walked into a spacious, white-walled consulting-room equipped to perfection. A dream! She would have given her right arm in the Dales to have had one like it. Nick leant against a desk, folding his arms, watching her as she looked around. Tracing his shadow out of the corner of her eye, she thought for the size of him how agile and economical in his movements he was.

What was going on in his mind now? The hairs on her neck stood on end as she felt his gaze. Why had he brought her here?

'Come and meet some of our boarders.' There it was again — another direct command disguised as an invitation!

'I don't think so, Nick. I really should be on my way — Don will be worrying.'

'He'll know where you are. Come on, we're heading for the climax of the tour, and you wouldn't want to miss the best part. We've some very interesting cases at the moment.'

She followed him, feeling cross that she was beguiled by her own curiosity and even crosser with him for finding her weak spot. One of many, she corrected herself, unable to take her eyes off the broad-shouldered back, the slim hips and strong athletic legs. Nick Lloyd — her teenage fantasy! His memory had always lain on the perimeter of her mind, inextricably mixed with the sensations of growing up. Surely she had grown out of it by now? The trouble was she had been working too hard! She had been engrossed in too many animal bodies to notice the human ones.

Giving her head a little shake, she made up her mind that this would be the last stop. After this, it was back home to Don and the comforts of the luxurious new bathroom and something to eat.

'Here we are.' The room was lit by night lights. The rosy glow and the body warmth of the animals and a few tiny grunts and snarls made Briony's insides tingle with excitement. Her eyes immediately fell on a large brindled dog lying curled in a roomy cage, his wet nose lifting to sniff their arrival.

'His name is Hercule,' Nick said, watching the direction of her eyes. He went to let him out. 'Hercule's a three-year-old greyhound, with an excellent temperament. Perhaps you'd like to examine him . . . and tell me what you think?'

Briony couldn't resist. She couldn't resist any animal, but Hercule looked adorable. He had glossy brown eyes and a proud muzzle, but his ears lay flat — because of pain? After petting him gently, she looked up at Nick. 'May I see you walk with him, please . . . in a circle around the room?'

45

Nick walked with him, Hercule obediently trotting to heel past the other recovery cages. After watching closely for a few minutes, Briony ran her fingers over the area she suspected harboured the problem. She discovered a warm, swollen area on the hind leg, and the animal jerked. 'As I haven't X-rays to go on and I don't know his history I would guess Hercule has been track racing. He was walking uncoordinatedly, and that's usually a sign of trouble.'

'So what would you say is the problem?'

She laid her fingers on the area. 'Here, there's a rupture . . . caused possibly by a direct blow . . . or maybe from extremely violent exercise. It's painful and swollen and very warm to the touch.'

Nick's black eyebrows raised in acquiescence. 'Like to have a stab at what we're doing?'

Briony laughed, her blue eyes creasing up. 'Do I get the impression you're testing me?'

46

He smiled wryly, watching her.

'Well . . . I'd guess Hercule was initially brought to you some weeks ago. Maybe his owner said he wasn't running well?'

Nick nodded, his mouth twitching a little at the corners as she made him wait for her answer.

'You advised rest,' she rattled off, teasing him no longer, 'but now it's obvious rest hasn't done the trick. You're going to perform a surgical repair within the next few days. After that, immobilisation of the limb for several weeks and perhaps some ultrasound therapy to reduce scar tissue during the healing phase. How will that do?'

'Ten out of ten.'

Briony jerked up her eyes towards him. 'I wouldn't be up to much if I couldn't diagnose something as simple as this.'

'Not that simple. Not for some. You had a hunch and you worked on it — something everyone in the medical profession should do.'

With the growing sensation that he was examining her every word and move she watched him guide Hercule back on to his warm blanket, equally flattered and puzzled by his attitude. With the devil in her she decided to add a little cachet to her diagnosis. 'I — er — don't suppose that's the last you'll see of Hercule, though.'

'Oh?' Nick tilted his head, walking back to her.

'These ruptures have a nasty habit of recurring in the same sites — I'm sure I'm not telling you anything you don't know already.'

'Do please carry on.' His eyes were shaded in the soft light. It was difficult to gain any satisfaction from showing off when you couldn't see a response!

'I saw quite a few of these injuries up north. Greyhounds are made to race at speed around a track in an anti-clockwise direction. Indeed, other breeds are encouraged now, especially in rural areas. Lameness is pretty widespread and I don't feel the public in general are aware of the troubles this sport generates . . . ' Her voice faded. She was on her soapbox. Nick was silent, his face in shadow. She felt herself shiver, aware that she had been doing most of the talking this evening — again!

'You obviously care very much about animals,' he said at last, moving across the room.

'Doesn't every vet?'

'To a certain degree . . . what would you say about our friend here?' In the blink of an eyelid he had opened another recovery cage and a black haystack padded towards her. 'Let me introduce Loppy; she's nine and carrying far too much weight.'

A deliciously warm pink tongue flicked over her ankle and, bending down, Briony was treated to a whiskery nuzzling around her ear. Somehow there seemed to be a stethoscope in her hand.

'Hello, Loppy. Come on, let's have a

look at you. Am I ever going to manage to get out of here?' she asked Nick, looking up at him with a rueful smile.

'You wouldn't want to miss the opportunity of listening to Loppy's functionings, would you?' His smile was so devastatingly spontaneous that she almost dropped the stethoscope. With some difficulty she cast her attention back to the cuddlesome mound of hair. She listened attentively to the combination of muscle contractions, the movement of blood indicating the opening and closing of the valves within the heart. Detecting the rhythmic 'lubb-dup', she moved the stethoscope. The lubb-dup, however, seemed oddly separated.

'Loppy has a murmur . . . it's quite noticeable if you listen for it. Have you done an ECG?'

Nick nodded, waiting.

Briony put down the stethoscope, checking for distension of veins or swelling of the abdomen. 'She has fluid accumulation — here, around the abdomen. And her lungs seem slightly congested. What did you find on the radiographs?'

'I'll leave you to tell me.'

Briony examined the radiographs as Loppy found her own way back to her bed. She hesitated, feeling the warmth of Nick's male presence beside her. Why did he make her so nervous? She cleared her throat purposefully. This was going to be the very last detour he dragged her on, despite the fact that she was thoroughly enjoying herself!

'The angiogram shows the dye passing through the catheter via the femoral artery and aorta to the left ventricle . . . but this is elementary; it's quite obvious . . . do you want me to continue?'

'Yes,' he nodded approvingly, 'please do.'

'You must be well aware of the inevitability of such a case. She's suffering from aortic stenosis. The ventricle has to increase its work to pump blood around the body. She's certainly very tired, indicating the inability of the heart to maintain systematic blood-pressure.'

'So what about treatment?'

She glanced at the dog, sleeping contentedly now. 'Loppy's nine, you say? She's probably had a very happy life, by the looks of her. Drug therapy will give her a temporary respite, but other than that . . . '

Nick smiled, seeming at last to be satisfied. 'Thank you. Most enlightening, and patiently delivered. Unfortunately, there isn't very much we can do, just drug therapy, as you've so correctly advised, and maybe take a look at her diet.'

'Has she any Newfoundland in her?' Briony asked as an afterthought. 'Aortic stenosis is sometimes a genetic defect in that particular breed.'

Even before he spoke his expression told her she had guessed correctly. 'The father was Newfoundland, the mother a Labrador.'

'Well . . . ' she gave a deep, satisfied sigh, edging towards the door ' . . . if you've no more life-and-death cases for me, I really must go now.'

Ignoring the hint of sarcasm in her voice, he traced her steps. 'Of course. I didn't realise it was so late. I'll see you to the door . . . and don't worry if you see my car gone in the morning. I'll pick it up early.'

For the first time that evening his fingers went up to the pad of gauze on his forehead and she saw the distinct passage of pain travel across his face. 'You'll need some pain-killers tonight,' she murmured softly as they walked into the corridor.

'I think I'll administer my own relaxant, in the form of a remedial glass of brandy, when I get home,' he smiled. But the smile had left his face when, at the glass doors, he swung back to her. She had a distinct feeling in her stomach that he was not going to allow her to leave without reminding her of the afternoon's catastrophe.

But she was quite wrong. It was far worse.

With faint mockery in his eyes he asked, 'Perhaps you wondered about our little discussion back there in the recovery-room?'

'I thought we were just talking shop.' Now her stomach was feeling like lead!

He nodded. 'We were indeed. You seem to have all your wits about you. You're concise, intelligent, you have deep, intuitive feelings for animals. As I've satisfied myself on all these counts, I want you to work for me — temporarily, of course, just until I sort myself out some decent staff. Don't look so surprised! Surely you had some idea of what I was leading up to?'

Briony felt her jaw open, astounded at herself for being so naïve. So he *had* been testing her! He wanted to see her mettle before offering her a job. 'You're not serious!' she gasped.

'Deadly serious. I wish I weren't! I'm desperate for staff at the moment. We just can't cover our areas and keep the small animal side up together. You're not committed; you told me so yourself. There's absolutely no reason why you shouldn't work here. And if it's money you're worried about, I can assure you a locum's salary is a very generous one.'

She felt the blood draining from her face as she remembered her eagerness to answer all those questions of his. Suddenly she felt so cross she could hardly see straight.

'Don't hold your breath like that, you'll pass out,' he told her calmly. 'So that's settled, then. I'll ring you over the weekend to finalise details.'

'I can't!' she blurted. 'I simply can't work for you!'

'Oh?' He looked at her with annoyed disdain. 'And why can't you?'

'For . . . for lots of reasons!'

'Name one.' He waited, rocking on heels, that impatient expression stealing across his face that she would have loved to see wiped off. But she was at a complete loss. In her panic and anger she couldn't think of one sensible reason for turning down the offer. She could say she didn't need the money, but that wasn't true. She had made up her mind to offer Don what capital she had as a loan so that he could get on his feet again. She would be left pretty broke. What would she do if she couldn't find work she liked or she simply couldn't find a job, full stop?

'I'm overwhelmed,' he rasped, raising his eyebrows, 'with your . . . reasons.'

'I'm afraid you'll have to take the answer as no — without explanations.'

He seemed impervious to this. 'You'll think rationally after a square meal and a good night's sleep.' He opened the door and a crisp breeze blew in, beckoning her out. 'I'll expect to see you here at nine on Monday morning.'

Feeling numb with anger, she was rooted to the spot. 'I very much doubt you will!'

The dark eyes became wry. 'That's more like the Briony Beaumont I remember of old . . . cursing her steed vociferously as it bolted towards the sandwich stall and not the winning post!' Opening the door to its full extent so that she was practically forced out, he added quickly, 'Oh, yes . . . just one more thing. I want a locum who'll cultivate a professional attitude towards her work, you understand. Most important! And I'll give you an added incentive just to prove what a reasonable man I am. Tell Don he can have his time . . . if I have yours.'

* * *

Her brother handed her a glass of ruby-red wine as with a tired sigh Briony related the last of her story sitting beside the drawing-room fire. The crisp jacket potatoes they had eaten for supper were just beginning to sustain her.

'I feel terrible, Bri, about all this. What can I say?'

She had had time to calm down. Nick's offer wasn't that bad, it was just the way he had gone about it, testing her out like that. She supposed if she hadn't been able to answer all those questions he would have dismissed her without a qualm! She gave a small giggle, thinking how gullible she'd been, rattling off her diagnosis, treatment and all.

'I'm glad you can see the funny side of it,' he groaned, looking surprised.

Don was depressed — he was taking this worse than she was! Perhaps she ought to make her decision now and be done with it? Though really there was no deciding. Working for Nick would solve all Don's problems until he sold Phoebe. 'I've made up my mind to accept Nick's offer. It's not such a crazy proposition — I need work, so what the heck?'

'But you can't be blackmailed, Bri! That's what it boils down to.'

She finished the last of her wine. 'It's just a temporary arrangement! I was just a bit peeved, I suppose, that Nick sprang it on me like that. Typical of an arrogant Lloyd.'

Don ran a hand through his hair.

'Nick and I have been getting along so well . . . it's all my fault . . . if I could settle my debts there wouldn't be this problem.'

Briony suddenly remembered her plan, though she felt too tired to elaborate tonight. 'I've had an idea, Don. Tomorrow we're going to get down to your accounts. I'm going to loan you some cash — it's only a couple of thousand, I'm afraid, but it will float you temporarily. Then you can pay me back when you're viable again.'

'No! Absolutely not!' Don's pale eyes sparked. 'I couldn't possibly let you do that.'

'Shut up, silly! Let's sleep on it. I'm nearly out for the count.'

He nodded, getting up wearily. 'I've made a bed up for you in the guest room. God, I wish Beth were here.'

'Stop fretting,' she advised gently. 'Worrying like this isn't going to help.' She brushed a kiss on his cheek.

Making her way slowly up the old oak staircase and along the landing, she gave in to a yawn, knowing her brother had no choice in accepting her offer. She was certain it would work out for him if he could just hang in over this rough patch . . . and she seemed to be his only hope.

Her room had a slanted roof, a lattice window and magnolia walls. Two years ago it had barely boasted a camp bed! Now there was a huge great one taking up most of the floor. Her cases stood in a corner. Could she manage to unpack them?

She walked to the bed, peeled off her clothes, and almost before her head reached the pillow she was asleep.

⋆   ⋆   ⋆

Nick phoned on Sunday, his voice businesslike. Briony didn't mind that; in fact she preferred it. A professional attitude was what he wanted — and that was exactly what he was going to get. He insisted on setting out the terms — a six-month contract and an immediate start. When he rang off, her head was banging like a drum!

On Sunday evening she cooked a roast. To her amusement, Don ate his with the appetite of a ravenous wolf and fell back satiated in his rocking-chair by the fire.

'That's the first real meal I've had since . . . '

Briony joined him with coffee. 'Since Beth left?'

He nodded. 'Three weeks ago.'

'Then isn't it time you got her back?'

'How? Tie and gag her and carry her across my shoulders? Her parents would have a fit. They'd probably ring the police if I showed up. My name's mud with them by now.'

Briony tapped the blazing fire with a poker, then studied the pensive, gentle male face as she advised, 'Do what you do with horses — be firm, have your way . . . make her a little scared of you!'

'But I wouldn't hurt a hair of her head!'

'And Beth knows it.' She sighed. Poor

Don, he was brilliant with horses but hopeless with feminine logic: 'You're too nice! Be a bit more machiavellian — women adore being put in their place once in a while.'

'The way our Nick did with you?'

Briony darted him a sharp glance. 'Certainly not! Whatever makes you say that?'

'Nothing. Well . . . quite a lot, actually. You came back on Friday night all sort of . . . oh, I don't know, I never did understand women. I'll never work the female sex out in a thousand years. One thing I do know, though — Father's going to have something to say about your sudden appearance. Don't you think you ought to call in and see him?'

Briony nodded. 'In a couple of weeks, maybe. I've had enough shocks for one weekend. I'll think of some excuse.'

He grinned. 'I hope you've got a good one ready regarding working for Nick. He won't like it at all.'

'I don't suppose he will.' She shrugged dismissively. 'But then Father hasn't ever approved of anything we've ever done . . . '

'But we've gone ahead and done it all the same,' Don laughed, his face crinkling in amusement.

And this will be no exception, thought Briony, thinking ruefully that she probably hadn't a clue as to what she was letting herself in for!

3

Briony arrived well before nine o'clock on Monday, just to be on the safe side. Nick's impatient manner over the phone had left her in no doubt as to what he expected.

It wasn't until Ben Hall waved that she began to feel better. Fair-haired and bearing a mischievous grin, the young vet introduced himself as he got out of his car. 'Pleased to have someone to tell my troubles to,' he joked, the grin spreading across his face.

'Do you have many of them?' Briony laughed, hoping she sounded a lot more confident than she felt as they walked to the surgery.

'I'm outnumbered by women . . . no offence, it's quite nice really. The girls are great, and Lea isn't bad. She's better once you get to know her. And if Nick's around she's all sweetness and light.'

'Oh . . . I see.' It was probably common knowledge that Nick and his pretty female assistant had something going between them.

'Not that there's anything in it,' Ben added unconvincingly. Opening the door, he asked, 'Nervous?'

'A little.'

'Don't be. When Nick phoned me last night to say we had our locum he was very complimentary.'

Briony raised her eyebrows. 'He was?' She didn't know Ben well enough to decide whether his line was pure flattery just to make her feel better.

The two resident nurses, Anita and Lorraine, greeted her warmly, and she would have enjoyed the introductions had she not glimpsed Nick's green BMW crunch to a halt in the car park. Through the window she saw his dark head, bearing a small dressing, some of the thick black hair falling over it. She took a deep breath, smiling at Lorraine. Why should he have this effect on her? She felt clammy with anticipation, the nerves in her stomach tightening. If anyone ought to be getting apprehensive it was Nick, for the way he had manoeuvred her!

He walked into Reception. Briony smiled. She wasn't going to let him get under her skin; in fact she was going to make the most of the job now she was here.

'Morning, everyone.' Nick returned her smile.

She watched as he chatted to the girls about the morning's appointments. He was dressed, unexpectedly, in a dark suit and a white shirt complemented by a strangely formal blue tie. Was the image for her benefit?

'How's the head?' she asked as he walked over to her. Her throat seemed to be constricting a little — nerves probably.

A tangy odour of aftershave met her nostrils as he stood by her. It had the disturbing effect of making her heart turn over inside her with a resounding flop.

'Great. Couldn't be better. You've met everyone, have you?'

'Oh, Lea's not in yet,' Anita volunteered. 'Mind, she was on call last night. Are you going to take open surgery, Nick? Ben's tied up with calls this morning.'

'How do you feel about taking it?' he asked Briony, as with that firm hand of his he guided her into the hall and down to Jack's room. 'Anita will be here to assist you, but I'll stay around if you like, just in case there are any hitches.'

Briony shook her head. 'You needn't bother, thanks all the same. The sooner I'm left to find my way around the better.'

They stood alone in the room. Little had she realised on Friday, when she had first seen it, that this was to be hers. It was a peculiar sensation. And perhaps Nick's attitude, perhaps the way he was dressed — and her own nervous apprehension — all added to

67

the atmosphere, making the going tougher.

'This afternoon you can come out with me and I'll break you in with some of our local farmers. There are a few cases I'd like you to familiarise yourself with — '

'Your rounds? But I was hoping I could concentrate on companion animals,' Briony interrupted in dismay. 'You mentioned that you only had one small animal vet, so naturally I assumed I'd be working with her.'

He rocked, just a little, on his feet, a characteristic of his she was beginning to know well. 'I'm afraid you assumed wrongly. And I'm sorry if I gave you that impression. Lea organises all the surgery work and you will, of course, in time, be able to get down to a normal routine. But at the moment I'm going to have to use you as a general factotum.'

Trying not to let her disappointment show, Briony avoided the critical gaze.

'There's no problem with that?'

She smiled. 'No. None at all.'

When Nick had left, she let out a huge sigh of relief. It would have been too much to hope that she was going to be allowed to concentrate on the small animal side, her chosen sphere. Not that she minded farm work, but being dragged out on the first day was hardly what she had envisaged.

Anita walked in as she was recovering. 'Frazzled already?'

'Oh, dear . . . do I look it?' Briony laughed shyly, thinking her expression must have been obvious.

'No, I'm only joking. You're doing fine. Are you up to meeting your first client?'

She nodded, changing swiftly into her fresh white coat. 'Make it a straight-forward one, will you? Something nice and easy, parvos or boosters?'

Anita shook her head, amusement in her eyes. 'No such luck. It's Mrs Hardy. She's — er — well, perhaps I'd better let you draw your own conclusions. Gertie, Mrs Hardy's chihuahua, has developed a phantom pregnancy . . . this time.'

Briony's blue eyes widened. 'This time? Do I gather Gertie has ongoing problems?'

'I'd say about every six months!' Anita disappeared in search of her client. A few minutes later an elderly lady appeared, her white hair framed by a floppy hat. She carried a large shopping bag. As it dropped open, a wet nose the size of a penny presented itself — snuggled in the bag was the tiniest chihuahua Briony had ever seen. At first glance there were no signs of even a spare tyre, let alone a phantom pregnancy!

'Gertie's sprouting out in all directions,' whispered Mrs Hardy, barely audible. Fragile fingers ran over the exposed tummy. 'Just look — rolls of fat. And she won't leave her toy alone. Cuddles it all the time, hatching it!' A green squeaky toy whined as Gertie bit malevolently into it with her tiny pincer teeth. It was clear that Gertie was

70

simply enjoying the attention. 'Dr Jack always put her right. Why can't I see him?'

Briony reached out for the tiny creature, only to retreat quickly as she snapped her disapproval. 'Er . . . I'm afraid he's in America for a while. What . . . what treatment exactly did he prescribe?'

'Prescribe?' Mrs Hardy looked horrified. 'He didn't prescribe, my dear . . . oh, no! Not pills. No! Gertie is green. She's as pure as the driven snow. He talked to her, you see. Psychotherapy, that's what Dr Jack did. Had her in for analysing. Something to do with her puppyhood.'

'I see,' Briony nodded, not at all sure she did. 'In that case . . . perhaps we'd better keep Gertie in for the day?'

'You wouldn't . . . put anything nasty into her dinner . . . you wouldn't do that?'

'Certainly not. I shall want her *compos mentis* for our chat.'

Mrs Hardy smiled, displaying two

neat rows of brown teeth. 'Excellent. Dr Jack would have said the same himself. Now, be a good girl, won't you, Gertie?'

The chihuahua bristled in Briony's gentle grasp, a growl that rumbled like a volcano zipping through the minuscule body. By the time Briony reached the recovery-room, settling Gertie with a saucer of milk, luckily no fingers had been severed.

'Will I be treating many more of our patients with analysis?' Briony asked Anita on her return. 'Dr Jack sounds as if he might have his own cult following.'

Laughing, Anita nodded. 'Oh, there's only one Mrs Hardy. Now nothing will seem impossible!'

'I'm relieved to hear it,' Briony grinned, the mention of the impossible bringing Nick back to mind. 'Oh, Anita, Nick has asked me to go on the rounds with him this afternoon. Do we have any spare wellingtons and jeans? I can hardly go like this.' She glanced down at her navy pencil-slim skirt and court shoes, an outfit she'd taken some time over selecting for her first day at work.

Anita took her to a cupboard. 'Take your pick. We're kitted out for any emergency. We have the laundry keep them fresh for us . . . even in Theatre we tend to get covered!'

Briony found herself some working clothes, a serviceable pair of jeans and an anorak. She wasn't going to be embarrassed by not being dressed properly!

The morning progressed without any hitches, her list coming to an end just before lunch. She shared sandwiches and coffee with the girls in the staffroom, though Lea's absence was conspicuous, especially as Briony had hoped to get to know her better. 'Perhaps I'll catch her tomorrow,' Briony observed, but by the look on the young nurse's face she couldn't help thinking getting to know Lea might take a little longer than a lunch break! Deciding it was best not to ply Anita with too many questions, she changed, packed her case and hurried to meet

Nick in the office.

'What have you got that stuff on for?' he asked, amusement in his voice.

'Won't I need it? I thought — '

'I didn't say we were going to be knee-deep in mud!'

'It has been raining . . . ' She peered out of the window at the damp grey skies.

'Up to you,' he murmured. Briony noticed he hadn't bothered to change, merely putting on his jacket over the suit. What an idiot she felt! Obviously he only wanted to introduce her to his clients to begin with.

As the phone rang, Briony was just about to say she would go and change back into her own clothes, but she was cut short by Nick's face darkening. 'It's someone for you. Says it's important he speak to you right away.'

'Did he give his name?' Who else apart from Don knew she was here? She certainly hadn't written to tell any of her close friends in Yorkshire yet.

Nick stared at her. 'He said his name

is Matthew Prior. He says you and he are . . . close friends.'

'Oh . . . Matthew — er — yes, he is, actually.' Taking the instrument, she sensed Nick was not going to move out of the office, nor in fact move more than a few steps away.

'Hello, Matthew.' She turned to look out of the window as she spoke, but she could feel Nick's eyes boring into her back. Matthew was an old friend, one of her father's colleagues. She hadn't thought to inform him of her move, so it was probably Greg Harding who had explained that she'd returned to Bagbourne. Possibly Matthew had phoned Don, for that was the only place he would get her number.

The call didn't take long; she was too aware of Nick's presence and the time factor. When she put the phone down she felt obliged to explain. 'Matthew's my father's business adviser. Ever since Father gave up the stables and concentrated on his City interests Matthew has helped out — he's a stockbroker . . . '

'So your father manages to keep tabs on you through him?'

She didn't like Nick's tone, nor the inference he had made. Matthew had been a good friend over the years, calling in to see her whenever he had business in the north, taking her out to dinner and keeping her filled in with family news. He'd always been neutral as regarded her relationship with her father, and for this reason she had been quite happy to see him. There was no romance between them, though he was an extremely good-looking man in his late thirties.

'I see Matthew from time to time. He's a good friend, no more than that.'

'I thought you said you had no commitments?' Nick persisted.

Briony's brows arched at his tone. She would not be bullied, nor would she be interrogated again! 'I don't term my friendship with Matthew as a commitment, not in the sense you mean. I came back to Bagbourne in order to find myself a practice, and, to be blunt, that's exactly what I intend to do once Don's debt is cleared up. That's my only commitment at the moment. But this is getting us nowhere, is it?' She took a small breath, calming herself. 'I think it's time we went, don't you?'

He shrugged. 'There's no rush. Have you had lunch?'

'Yes, thanks, with the girls.'

'No problems in open surgery?'

'Not exactly a problem . . . more a diversion. Mrs Hardy?'

'Ah.' She was relieved to see a smile touch his mouth, mellowing the hard lines that had formed on his face during the telephone call. It had been a tense interlude, especially as she had stood up for herself, but fortunately he seemed to have taken it well. 'Mrs Hardy and Gertie . . . how did you manage? What was it this time?'

'A phantom pregnancy. I've promised to talk Gertie out of it. She's in for counselling.'

Nick chuckled, his eyes glimmering

darkly. It was amazing, the change in his face when he let himself go and relaxed. She would like to see more of that warmth. Surely he had social interests to alleviate work? Her curiosity whetted, Briony wondered where the delectable Lea came into his life.

The BMW ate up the road, though he was a careful driver. She felt her heart race as they left Bagbourne behind and entered the countryside, the drizzle damply glistening on the trees, the burning colours of autumn enhanced by rain. 'I'd forgotten just how intoxicating the countryside is here . . . ' she whispered almost to herself.

'Which is another reason why I've brought you out today.'

She looked at him, puzzled. 'I'm sorry? I'm not quite with you.'

His features softened as he said, 'To remind you of all you've been missing. To be quite honest, I thought bringing you out to the sticks would make a far better impression than staying in all day. You know what they say about first impressions, don't you?'

She laughed lightly, wondering if that applied to human relationships. And if so, what could be said for theirs? She was to wish several hours later, after being introduced to some of Nick's more affluent clients, that she had presented a better first impression herself! Jeans and wellingtons and a baggy anorak didn't exactly fit the part of the group's new locum. When they left a rather grand country house where she and Nick had been invited on afternoon stables with the owner, she said as much to Nick.

Surprisingly he shrugged off her comment. 'I shouldn't worry. You look great to me.' He took his eyes fleetingly from the road. 'How on earth do you manage to keep all that coppery hair so shiny? It's even more eye-catching than I remember. I was always mesmerised by it.'

Briony felt herself blush fiercely, her hand automatically going up to tidy the wilful curls which persistently spiralled out of the hairband. The strange thing was, compliments from Nick didn't quite seem like compliments.

'Now we'll visit a couple of farms,' he said without giving the matter another thought. 'They're large acreage with dairy cows and pigs, all top-notch stock. We had a bad fright with mastitis early in the summer, so I keep a vigilant eye on Henry Dappledale's herd of Friesians.'

Briony settled back, watching the hedgerows whip by. Nick could switch from a light tone to a professional mood without turning a hair. But she rather liked that. There was no safer subject than work, and perhaps after their harrowing start the future might present a more equable prospect.

Dappledale Farm lay sleepily in a hollow of chestnut trees, its green pastureland spreading out in a triangle across the slopes of the countryside. Henry Dappledale, pleased to show off his herd of Friesians, nevertheless was preoccupied with his calves.

'Too loose, too wet!' he complained to Nick as he prodded a manure pile. 'I'm worried it's scouring.'

Nick looked over the calves as Briony watched. He'd changed into wellingtons, a spare pair from the boot, but even so, to Briony's horror, muck had attached itself to his trousers.

'Any blood?' she heard Nick ask.

'Not yet.'

They walked from the pen into daylight. 'I'll come up the day after tomorrow,' Nick told Henry. 'If you've any problems before, ring me.'

'Don't need to tell us that!' muttered the red-faced man, his cap shading small, astute eyes. 'Don't want scouring after the mastitis.'

Briony remained quiet, realising they had caught the farmer at a worrying moment. By the time they got back in the car, Nick's trousers were covered in mud spats. She looked at him wryly, hoping the amusement didn't show on her face.

As he drove, he went over the case of

Mr Medlicott and his pigs, their next call. The herd, running free range, were the farmer's obsession. 'Medlicott's besotted by Seth and Sarah,' Nick told her with a grin. 'His sow and his boar are Large Whites, both pretty old now, but Sarah dotes on Medlicott. He bottle-fed her from a week old, and she follows him around like a dog.'

When Nick's BMW hummed into the yard, Mr Medlicott was under way with his chores, a large pinky-white pig rooting beside him. Knowing just how strong pigs were, Briony cautiously left the car, remembering several occasions where she had been tipped up by a bolting animal.

'Sarah won't hurt you.' Mr Medlicott shook her hand warmly. 'She's as human as you or I.'

'I can see that,' Briony smiled, watching the lazy actions of the farmer's companion, nose glued to the weeds. But she still wasn't too sure. Pigs, she knew, were a little like donkeys — a law unto themselves.

'Better brains on 'em than dogs, did you know that?' The farmer scratched his pig's back with a bristled broom, then tipped a bucket of water over the rough skin.

Nick stood back, but the spray caught his trousers. Faintly disturbed, he asked, 'What about those sores on your new pigs? Did they develop?'

The farmer, unaware of the effects of the dousing, tipped yet another bucket. 'Not too sure. They seem to have gone. Can't be certain, though. I haven't let Sarah near them; she's due to farrow any time now. Expect at least ten from her ... don't want to court trouble while she's suckling.'

Briony observed the swollen under-carriage, Sarah's maternity equipment hanging readily in plump pink upside-down mountains.

'Something's got her nose!' Mr Medlicott warned as Sarah lifted her huge head, her deep-set piggy eyes assessing what was going on in the yard. 'If she gets a sniff of something

83

she doesn't like, she'll be off, so watch it!'

The warning came too late, though not for Briony, who jumped smartly to one side, sensing Sarah's disquiet. Nick moved fractionally slow. The great body hurtled past him, sending him flying. Briony was dimly aware of a windfall of mud and Mr Medlicott's yard hose winding itself around the long legs of her employer as though it had a life of its own.

'Damn that sow!' The farmer was off at speed, yelling curses, leaving Briony to help Nick, who was floundering with the hose, endeavouring to ease himself out of the foul-smelling mud into which he had slipped. She tugged at a sleeve, the only clean piece of cloth that seemed to be left. Nick growled under his breath, trying to step up. But his weight was too much for her, and before she could steady herself she too was falling.

She landed in the mud too, the cold, wet sensation of gurgling brown liquid seeping instantly through her pants, covering the palms of her hands and spattering on to her face. She turned to see Nick in much the same condition, sitting beside her, grinning.

'Is this where I say we shouldn't keep meeting like this?' His laughter was deep and rich, and it so surprised her that for a moment she just sat in silence. Then she too was laughing, watching the handsome, dirty face opposite her. Somehow, sitting in the mud in Mr Medlicott's yard was about the best thing that had happened to her all day, the release of laughter easing out the tension and stiffness from her body.

She hardly realised he had slipped an arm around her shoulders. 'I think I owe you an apology,' he murmured, his voice husky, his dark eyes smiling. 'A big one.'

'You do?'

He chuckled again. 'It was I who wore the wrong clothes, not you. In fact, you made an extremely sensible choice.' Their laughter subsided and his face was serious, the amusement fading from his eyes, to be replaced with an intensity that almost frightened her.

The fingers on her shoulder tightened, her body going hot and tingling under his touch. By some mysterious feat of movement she was taken slowly into his arms. She gazed up at him, her eyes wide open, and her limbs felt powerless, her heart beating so rapidly that she had to swallow. He drew her closer, into the rock-solid hardness of his chest. His breath fanned on her cheek.

A tremor ran through her body as his mouth came to within an inch of her own. She saw his face mistily for a few seconds, astounding herself with the need that coursed through her veins. Then there was no hesitation, no doubt in his kiss as he parted her lips and enquired at first lightly into her mouth, teasingly almost and then with an urgency that rocked her. Her muscles, her backbone softened with heady pleasure. She yearned to be able to throw her arms around him, to respond as she wanted, but a small corner of her brain resisted the temptation. What was she supposed to do? She knew what she wanted to do! Then, as if in answer to her silent question, he took hold of her chin and softly eased her face away, searching her eyes with his. For miserable seconds she was suspended, thinking he was amused. Was it mockery in those dark, unreadable eyes? As she stared back at him, her eyes hazy with confusion, his fingers became hard and insistent around her jaw. Even if she had wanted to move she couldn't! His grip was like a vice. Her mind lay trapped, unfocused; rational thoughts other than those of the moment were impossible.

What was he thinking? Why was he looking at her like that? Then, achingly slowly, he drew her face towards him and her lids shut down as he kissed her again. She wanted to savour every sensation, indulge in the fantasy that seemed to be swamping them. With total desertion of logic, she imagined being lifted, higher and higher, until it seemed her heart might burst from the altitude. Her arms curled around the taut, muscled neck and she felt him groan softly into her mouth as her fingers spread themselves languorously in his hair. She had wondered what his kiss would be like, and now she knew. Eyes closed and breathing in his taste, she felt the sensual seduction of his mouth overwhelm her.

'She's vanished, damn and blast! Perishing pig's a lunatic!'

The farmer's oath luckily reached them before he did. Recoiling, giddy with emotion as though she had been drinking champagne, Briony tried to scramble to her feet, catching the red face of Mr Medlicott coming around the corner. She glanced back at Nick. He was on his feet too, the contours of his face hardening as though he had just woken up and discovered the unpleasant reality of his circumstance.

She put up her hands to feel the abrasiveness of drying mud on her cheeks and the flush underneath that had nothing at all to do with drying dirt.

'I thought you said that pig was supposed to be human?' Nick bit out at the farmer, who looked at them in surprise.

'She is . . . more often than not.' The farmer gave a chuckle. 'You two look as though you've been run over by a tractor.'

A cry from the farmhouse saved Nick from the embarrassment of answering.

'Sarah's at the veggie garden! Sniffs out potatoes like old socks! You two'll have to see yourselves out . . . '

Briony realised her heart was still thumping as the farmer hurried off. She dreaded Nick looking at her, dreaded seeing the shut-off in his eyes. She looked under her lashes at him, trying to recover from the faint tingle of delight she felt inside as she thought of that kiss.

'I think it's time we made a move,' he said abruptly, making a cold shiver go down her spine at his change in attitude. 'Leave our good friend to his swine-catching.' He took her arm as they crossed the yard. She said nothing as she felt his body tensing beside her. When they arrived at the car, before she could get in he put his large hand on the door, barring her way. 'Look, about what happened back there . . . '

Briony gazed up into the dark eyes. They were cool and remote, and she had the feeling she'd made a huge mistake this afternoon. She sensed his reluctance to bring up the subject. That was understandable — after all, he'd kissed her through an accident! There was no need for an apology — if he was going to offer one. It had taken two to make a kiss like that!

'Let's forget about it, Nick, shall we? Put today down to . . . experience?'

She'd uttered sensible words, a remark that saved him — and herself — from further embarrassment. But the

sensible observation was not the truthful one. Her knees went weak as she
looked to him for a response. There was
none as his eyes flicked over her, white
edges of teeth revealed in between
straight lips.

A professional attitude at all times
had been his demand on Friday, and it
seemed he meant it, though he himself
had made an error today. Was she really
supposed to forget about it, pretend it
never happened?

A look crossed his face that she
couldn't interpret — it was probably
relief! He opened the car door and
wordlessly allowed her to settle into her
seat.

'Let's forget about it, Nick, shall we?'
she had followed up with, very gener-
ously, very sensibly. But her mind
persisted in going over the afternoon
again and again during the journey
home. Nick's effort at sketches of
conversation briefly caused her to
surface from her thoughts and make a
reply. But she couldn't stop herself

from thinking. Her life had been a busy one, sometimes hectic and always fulfilling. It was still all these things, but something else had been added when he kissed her today. Something she had never experienced before.

'Almost home,' he said.

'Yes, very nearly.'

'I'll — er — make sure you have your share of surgery work this week.' He turned the car into the drive. 'In fact I'll speak to Lea about it and Ben too. I'm sure a rota can be worked out.'

'I'd prefer you didn't go to any trouble on my behalf. I'm quite happy to fit in.'

Briony realised how politely they had been talking. Superficially the last hour had been their most civilised.

All because of five minutes on the ground in Mr Medlicott's yard!

4

When Matthew rang early on Friday morning, Briony took the call in the office.

She had asked Matthew not to ring her at work, and he'd apologised, saying he'd obtained her number from Don and, since he was standing in an airport lounge at the time before boarding a flight to Brussels, he'd telephoned her directly.

'Come out to dinner tomorrow evening . . . and I'm not taking no for an answer!' he told her.

Had he planned catching her at work, knowing she would agree in an effort to get him off the phone? And she'd done precisely that, accepting his invitation quickly, watching Nick climb out of his BMW in the car park.

'Prior, was it?' Nick strolled in, a gleam in his eye as he watched a flush

93

creep into her face. It was the first time she'd found herself alone with him since Monday, and she was suddenly conscious of the nagging ache inside her. All week she'd refused to pursue her feelings towards him, telling herself the sensations he had aroused in her would disappear.

For the last few days she had barely seen him, their busy paths running in opposite directions, and she'd managed to do a fair job of sweeping her emotions under the carpet. Whatever they were, this was certainly not the time to air them!

'As a matter of fact,' she answered huskily, 'it was Matthew. I've asked him not to call me at work . . . I'm sorry. I know you — '

'It doesn't matter, don't apologise. I'm not the ogre you obviously think I am.' Nick studied her, laying down his case and taking off his coat. This morning he had a mild growth of beard about his chin, although it was clear he had shaven. There had been an outbreak of swine vesicular disease and he had been working long hours with the Ministry officials. It had taken its toll; the lines in his face told her that. He smiled, the tiredness showing.

She managed a smile too, relaxing. 'I just had the impression you weren't terribly keen on him.'

He shook his head, the wound on his forehead a healing scab now. 'I don't know the guy. But he certainly seems keen to pin you down, for someone who's only a friend . . . do you know he's phoned several times this week?'

Briony jumped. 'No one mentioned that!'

'I'm sorry, I should have. It was me he talked to. I naturally assumed he'd contacted you at Don's.'

Now she knew Matthew was up to something. 'Perhaps he rang and couldn't get an answer.'

'Perhaps. He's the persistent kind, isn't he?'

As it was said with humour, Briony

nodded, smiling. 'I'm seeing him tomorrow. I'll tell him to stop jamming our business line.'

Nick moved to the desk, sorted a few papers busily. 'Dinner, is it?'

She nodded, moving to the door. 'Dinner . . . and a chat over old times. Nothing more.'

He looked up, the dark eyes fanned by thick black lashes. 'You deserve a break . . . it's been quite a week for us all.'

Curiouser and curiouser. Was he trying to put himself out to be pleasant? If so, he was doing a remarkably good job — so much so, she almost believed him! Could his attitude be a direct result of Monday's episode at Medlicott's? Was he trying to atone, feeling guilty about the way he had kissed her after telling her he expected a professional attitude?

Involuntarily she took a deep, shaky breath as she thought of that kiss and the way he had held her. She remembered the look in those jet eyes

— and how it had evoked a response in her.

'I'd better get started,' she told him abruptly, keeping her eyes at a safe level and avoiding his. Slipping out of the room, she wondered hectically what he must think. She was behaving ridiculously. Surely she could handle the situation without behaving like a child?

Deep in thought, she almost collided with Lea. As Briony glanced back, the door of the office shut firmly in her face. Lea and Nick alone. The soft murmurings behind the door sent a stab of pain into her ribs. Telling herself she had better snap out of this mood, she began her list and forced herself to concentrate.

Her first two patients were straightforward parvos, but her third was a small mongrel dog who looked very sick indeed. 'Peter's swallowed a pebble. It was yesterday on his walk,' the elderly owner explained. 'I saw him playing with it, and before I could stop him he gave a great gulp.'

'Has he been in pain for long?' Briony examined the dog's abdomen gently.

'I'm afraid so. I was just hoping it would pass through him.'

'I think we'll have to take an X-ray and see what the result is.'

A short while later, with reluctance, Briony explained that she would have to operate. When Mr Greene had gone, she turned to Anita, glancing at her watch. 'Please prepare one of the theatres as quickly as you possibly can . . . I don't want to lose a minute with this little fellow.'

Anita hesitated, her eyes shifting. 'I'm afraid I shall have to see Lea first . . . '

'Why?' Briony asked. 'I won't need to trouble Lea. You're qualified to assist me, aren't you?'

'Yes . . . but Lea has given orders that she must be consulted before you . . . before surgery.'

'But why?' Briony asked again. 'None of the theatres are being used, are they?'

Anita's embarrassed silence spoke

volumes. Lea, for some reason, did not want Briony to operate. For whatever reason, Lea had taken a dislike to her, it was obvious.

Briony said softly but firmly, 'Go straight to Theatre with Peter. I'll meet you there. Don't worry about telling Lea; I'll see her myself.' But she had a feeling it would be better to operate first, leaving any questions to be answered later, and, resolving to sort the matter out when the dog was safely delivered of its stone, she hurried along to scrub up.

In Theatre, Peter's scrawny little body luckily harboured a courageous heart. Anita monitored the anaesthesia, her attention divided between the respiration and Briony's instructions. A pebble had lodged in the narrowest region, the jejunum, and Briony was quick to make a deft incision and find it. Using forceps to place the offending article in a dish for Anita to see, she sighed with relief. 'No wonder he was feeling sorry for himself. This must have caused him a lot of pain.'

Checking her patient's breathing and heartbeat, Briony was suddenly aware of being watched. Turning around, she saw a pair of tense violet eyes surveying her. Lea must have come into the theatre at some point. Well, what did it matter? She was almost through now, though she would have to make sure Peter was into recovery before committing her attention to what looked like her first altercation with another member of staff.

'Thanks, Anita . . . ' Briony watched the young nurse for a response as she peeled off her gloves. It came in the brief widening of her eyes, warning her that Lea was going to be difficult.

'May I ask you who gave you permission to begin surgery?' Lea demanded after Peter had been removed to a recovery cage.

Briony felt anger prickle her skin. Why had Nick's assistant taken such a dislike to her? There had hardly been enough time for a personality clash, surely?

'I didn't think I needed permission to save a life, Lea. I was doing my job, that's all.'

'You know exactly what I mean. I gave Anita strict instructions that I was to be informed if any surgery was to be embarked on.'

'Anita did as I told her.'

Lea took a pace forward, glaring at them both. 'She had express orders to come to me.'

'Was that really necessary?' Briony calmly removed her gown. 'I told Anita I'd see you, but I decided to get the surgery on its way as quickly as possible.'

'You had no right!' began Lea, only to be halted by a fresh voice, causing all three women to spin round.

'Thank you, Anita, that will be all.' Nick stood by the theatre doors, his eyes cautiously surveying them. 'Though if you'll come back to check your patient in about ten minutes, please?'

By the look on his face he wasn't happy about what he'd heard, Briony thought in dismay. The young nurse looked helplessly at her as she went out.

Nick moved across the room, his dark brows carving shadows on his cheeks. 'What on earth's going on? An operating theatre isn't the place to have a free-for-all.'

Lea flashed Briony a glance, then shrugged at Nick. 'It wasn't anything. A professional disagreement, that's all.'

His eyes questioning, he drove his hands deeply into his pockets. 'If either of you have problems regarding small animal work, I would very much appreciate it if you came to me before starting a squabble.'

'I'm sorry, Nick.' Lea smiled apologetically, turning towards Briony. 'Just a misunderstanding, then?'

Briony's eyes widened in surprise. Was Lea really putting on an act in front of Nick? She could hardly believe that a few minutes ago Lea had been rounding on her like a tigress.

Lea walked slowly to the doors of the theatre, casting a stiff smile at Briony. 'We usually try to make a point of not treading on one another's toes by double booking. Come and have a word with me any time you want to book the theatre. There won't be a problem.'

When Lea had gone Nick looked at Briony with a wry grin. 'She's trying to be friendly, you know.'

Briony knew exactly what Nick meant, but she wasn't so sure Lea did! Should she tell him about the way Lea had reacted to her operating? It was probably best to swallow on her pride and say nothing.

In her own room ten minutes later, she took a deep breath, feeling weary. The day had held promise and she had actually enjoyed herself. To have it complicated by friction with Lea was just what she'd wanted to avoid.

When Nick strolled in after her, her heart gave one of the odd little jerks she was taking for granted as a symptom of her nervous apprehension in his presence. He sat down, regarding her quietly. 'What happened between you two? What's all the fuss really about?'

Briony shook her head, trying to gather herself. 'No fuss to speak of . . . but if you want my honest opinion, I think Lea has taken a dislike to me.'

'That's absurd! She barely knows you. I rather thought she was putting herself out to be friendly.'

Briony bit her lip. He must be blind not to see Lea's antagonism!

His cheeks were taut with impatience. 'She's a promising vet, Briony. But she's had far less experience than you and she's probably feeling threatened at the moment. As far as I can see she's meeting you halfway. Now why can't you do the same . . . for harmony's sake?'

Briony gulped back her anger. This was the bitterest pill she'd had to swallow all week! Nick hadn't an earthly what was going on under his nose. The last person, however, to put him right was her. He would just think it sour grapes and write her off as another 'breed' of inflexible, intolerant women vets.

She listened in silence as he went on. 'Lea does all the organising of the operations simply because she's here and she knows what's what. The rest of us have our calls to make, which naturally leaves her to that particular job. You'll get used to the system in time.'

Formalities had to be observed, they were intrinsic in one's training — she understood that. But unfortunately Greg had given her her head. Left to her own devices, she had almost taken over in the last few years, knowing there was no one to interrupt her mode of working. In this case, she was going to have to accept Lea's authority — it wasn't that she minded. It was Lea's animosity which was so upsetting. Why was she hostile, and why the subterfuge in front of Nick?

He stood up, smiling down at her.

'Anyway, I'm not here to split hairs . . . how do you feel about helping me with Dappledale's calves this afternoon? I'm afraid they're scouring.'

Drawing a long breath, she tried to think of a way she wouldn't have to go. Not that she minded scouring calves; it was being alone with Nick again that perturbed her. 'How about Ben; isn't he available? I've several appointments, you see.'

'Ben's on a mastitis case. I'll be forever and a day with only one pair of hands.' Nick grinned, his eyes warm. 'I'm sure Lea will agree to fitting in your appointments.'

Briony imagined Lea would only be too pleased to see the back of her! Although maybe . . . 'What about asking Lea?' she volunteered. 'She doesn't get much opportunity for a change of scene; perhaps she'd appreciate the offer to go with you?'

His eyes were twinkling as he shook his head. 'Lea doesn't have much of a rapport with cows and sheep. I think it's safe to say she'd prefer taking your patients.'

Ten minutes later Briony found herself in Nick's car, whether she liked it or not. He eyed her speculatively. 'No problems?'

'No. Lea has taken my appointments.'

'I told you so. She can be very obliging.'

Briony refrained from saying Lea had barely lifted her head from a book she was reading in the staffroom!

'I see you've come prepared.' Nick glanced down at her jeans, her own property this time, ones she had brought in especially.

'And you too.' She smiled as she thought of Nick's mud-splattered suit. Had he really worn the suit just to make an impression? Now he wore navy cords, boots and a thick Aran jumper.

'Come on . . . share the joke!' His lips twisted in a smile as the car gathered speed, his strong fingers stroking the wheel.

Briony could hardly repeat what she was thinking, so she told him about one old farmer she'd had as a client in the Dales. She'd discovered him in his field one day with a lamb, telling her it was 'dead, or as near as damn it'.

'It was my first week of practice, actually. I was over-eager, and he was as hard as nails and not a lover of women vets.'

She turned to look at Nick as he was concentrating on the road. She liked the way his mouth curved when he was listening. A warm feeling came over her as he turned his head and their eyes met. Then, awkwardly, she found herself stringing words quickly together to get over the sensation. 'Actually we became quite good friends . . . he bet me ten pounds I'd not revive his lamb.'

'And you won the bet?'

'We took it back to the farmhouse. I wrapped the poor little thing in my fleece-lined anorak, because I guessed it was freezing. When I dried it out with a towel and there was a flicker of a heartbeat I knew luck was on my side.'

'And the farmer thought it was starving, I'll bet?'

Briony's eyes sparkled in amusement; she knew the mistake was a common enough one even for seasoned stock-men. 'He didn't realise it was only four hours old and hypothermia had taken place due to the high rate of heat loss during its drying out.'

The gates of the farm approached and Nick slowed down, taking the bumpy road with caution. When they came to a halt he turned fully round in his seat to look at her. Her heart gave one of those silly jerks and she swallowed hard.

'What happened?' he asked, his dark eyes roving her face.

'By chance I had an electric fan with me in the car and I dried the lamb out for a good couple of hours. The farmer thought I was quite mad, but suddenly I got a response and so I gave it a feed with a stomach tube. After the next feed I put him back with his mother and he began to suck immediately.'

'And so the word got round?'

'Unfortunately, yes.'

'Why unfortunately?'

'No one would lay bets with me after that. I was quite disappointed!'

He laughed aloud, ducking his head to peer out for the farmer. 'I'll remember not to lay you any wagers!'

Briony didn't have a chance to enjoy the warmth of his laughter, for Henry Dappledale came hurrying up to them, shaking his head worriedly. 'I thought you'd never get here. I've been waiting all day!'

Briony listened patiently as she got out. Farmers were farmers everywhere. When they were on top of the world everyone knew it; when they weren't there was hell to pay! And usually the vet did!

She worked quietly alongside Nick, administering the sick calves with an electrolyte and glucose preparation added to a quantity of warm water. Of the calves which were affected, half refused to drink.

'We're going to pass the stomach tube down, Henry,' Nick told the farmer, demonstrating the technique on a calf. 'You see, very slowly does it.'

He turned with a smile to Briony. 'I'll leave you to that one over there. Henry, go with Miss Beaumont, and watch every move she makes.'

'You've done this 'afore,' the farmer pronounced, a smile of satisfaction passing over his face as he watched her.

'A few times. You'll find it easy enough once you've done one yourself.'

The afternoon passed quickly after this, and by the time they finished Briony's hair was falling in untidy straw-flecked shadows on her shoulders. With a face devoid of make-up she saw the last calf back into its pen.

'Looks like a schoolgirl and works like a man,' Henry Dappledale muttered, walking off to see Nick. That comment, she decided with a feeling of great satisfaction, was as near a compliment as she would get.

'When you're finished come up to the house for tea,' she heard him telling Nick. 'And don't say no — Missus won't hear of it.'

After he had gone Nick chuckled beside her. She watched him draw his shirt-sleeves down over muscular fore-arms dusted in small black hairs. A roller-coaster feeling in her stomach took off, and she quickly wrenched her eyes back to his face.

'I've been out here many times, and that's the first occasion he's ever mentioned the missus, let alone tea.' Nick pulled on his jacket.

'Curious about a woman vet, I'd guess,' she managed, spellbound by her imagination. Did those fine black hairs really creep all over his body?

'There are advantages to being a woman,' he was musing beside her. 'Do you think if I wear a dark coppery wig next time, and high heels, I'll get myself another invitation?'

Knowing that no amount of decora-tion would camouflage the heady sense of masculinity that always came over her with Nick, Briony gave in to a burst of laughter. 'You could try . . . but somehow I can't imagine you in drag . . . you haven't the poise!'

'In that case, how fortunate I am to have a locum who uses her wiles to get us into the sanctum of sanctums.'

Laughing, they walked together in the late afternoon to the farmhouse with the smell of a wood-burning stove tingling their nostrils.

* * *

'Briony — you look too good for your own safety!'

Matthew's remark, *passé* though it was, justified the last two hours Briony had spent on her appearance. She'd hastily shopped during the afternoon for a dress, the Saturday rush in Bagbourne centre overwhelming enough to make her choice rash — sleek dark blue off-the-shoulder evening gown and a pair of high-heeled slingbacks, articles she would probably hide away in wraps until another rare visit to somewhere special.

And Chez Françoise was special. She'd heard about it from Anita, who had been taken there by her boyfriend on the opening night at the beginning of summer. According to Anita you needed a French dictionary at least, if not a helpful waiter.

Briony took in Matthew's solid form waiting on the doorstep. Still very blond, he brushed his hair with the expertise of an older man into a short, no-nonsense cut, adding authority to the Slavonic features. Handsome, yes . . . but not in the same sensual way as Nick.

Sensual? The word plundered her mind as she stared at Matthew. Did she really think Nick sensual?

'Briony . . . are you OK?' Matthew was staring at her, his blond eyebrows raised questioningly.

She gulped, telling herself to wake up. What was she doing thinking about Nick on her day off, on her one night's gay abandon ... with a man who turned many a woman's head, as she'd discovered before?

'Naughty girl, not telling me you'd decided to come back home,' Matthew reproached as he drove to Chez Françoise. The car was a large and deliciously comfortable Mercedes ... she could almost doze!

'Not home, Matthew,' she emphasised. 'You do understand that? I'm not going back to Amberfields.'

Matthew shrugged, his immaculate dark suit making him look the picture of elegance at the wheel. But she wouldn't forget he was her father's business adviser first and her friend secondly.

He chose to ignore her remark. 'You're looking stunning, Briony — can I take it you bought that dress especially for our date tonight?' She jumped, as suddenly his hand snaked across from the wheel, taking her wrist. Then his fingers intrusively slipped down between hers. It was the first time he had ever made such a movement — or described their meeting as a 'date'. What had happened since she last saw him? she wondered, almost panic-stricken. What had gone on to make him think this was anything more than their meetings usually were? Had her father something to do with it? Perhaps Nick had been right when he had loosely warned her he was keeping tabs.

The meal at Chez Françoise, an exclusive and highly expensive cordon bleu restaurant, was all Briony imagined it to be, though her mind wasn't so much on what she was eating as on her companion's behaviour.

With their backs to mirrored walls and sitting in half-moon, lushly upholstered chairs, they ate *champignons* in wine, sauté chicken and a sweet so light that she could barely distinguish the puréed strawberries from the meringue and thick, succulent cream.

As they drank glasses of black coffee afterwards tinged with liqueur, she rested back, wondering if Matthew would finally get around to what he had obviously been dying to say. She had known him for three years, and in all that time he had never acted the way he had tonight. His grey eyes had never left her. She had managed to glance in one of the mirrors, wondering if she'd grown horns, such was his attentiveness. But no, her red hair, curled up into a chignon, was just the same as ever. His gaze fell on her breasts, revealed roundly by the low neckline.

'It was a perfect meal, Matthew,' she said, arching her fine eyebrows and drawing back his attention. 'Thank you.'

'A penny for your thoughts, or should I offer a beautiful woman — a woman whom I've always admired — something a little more to her liking?'

Briony's smile faded as she glanced at Matthew across the table. He was deadly serious!

She stiffened involuntarily, desperate to change the subject. 'I was thinking how happy I was to be back here in Bagbourne, actually.'

'You mean at Nick Lloyd's?' His grey eyes hardened.

'I was referring to Bagbourne, Matthew, but actually, now you mention it — '

'You're happy to be home. It's natural enough,' he interrupted guardedly. 'After all, this is where you were born; the place will always be very special to you. But I'm glad too, Briony, for different reasons. You see . . . I'd really like to get to know you better. I've always felt — well, let's just say I've respected your independence, because I didn't ever want you to think I was your father's mouthpiece.'

So this was the first step towards the truth, even though he wasn't admitting to it. She liked Matthew. She didn't want to spoil things. Didn't he know that?

With a jerk of surprise she realised too late that his hand had grasped hers across the table. His fingers stroked the soft skin of her fingers . . . she couldn't pull away. She didn't want to seem ungrateful, and she did like him, but this was not what she wanted.

'Briony, I have to tell you, I've grown very fond of you over the years . . . very fond indeed.'

'But Matthew — '

'We get on well, we've so much in common. Our tastes are enormously compatible. Why shouldn't we let what we have between us deepen? Trust me, Briony. I know I could make you a very happy woman.'

Briony gave a small gasp as he leaned across the table and swiftly touched her lips with his own. Stunned, she sat quite still, feeling the colour flood into her cheeks. What could she say without hurting his feelings? How could she tell him her tastes were not at all his? Oh, she liked to pass an evening or two with him just as they had done in the past, but she had no interest in the stock market or the busy life of the City. She was a vet. Her life revolved around animals. Once, when he'd visited her at Greg's, a dog had salivated on his immaculate suit. He had gone quickly to his car, produced another pair of trousers and changed! At the time Briony had been merely amused; now she blanched at the thought. No, Matthew's tastes and hers were worlds apart!

With her head spinning, Briony mumbled that she really ought to find the powder-room. He looked irritated, the pale skin reddening slightly under duress. She left the table, forcing herself to go slowly. She wanted to run. In fact, given half a chance her long legs, like those of Phoebe, were aching to bolt. But she ascended the stairs carefully towards the small pink door — then stopped. Her heart almost jerked out from behind her ribcage.

A beautiful, dark-haired woman in a jade dress stood with her companion, obviously just about to leave.

Briony blinked and blinked again, unable to believe her eyes.

'An enjoyable meal?' Lea asked, her violet gaze swiftly flashing back to Matthew.

'Y-yes, wonderful, thank you,' Briony stammered, her face feeling as though it was on fire.

She stood, her heart palpitating, as Nick gave her a curt nod, helping Lea on with her coat. His eyes fixed her with such coolness, she couldn't move.

Had he seen Matthew kiss her? And what if he had — did it matter? Did it really matter that once again Nick would get the wrong impression completely?

Lea slipped her arm through Nick's. 'Have a good time,' she said in a sultry voice and, looking towards Matthew, added, 'I admire your taste . . . he is rather gorgeous, isn't he?'

And before Briony could think of a reply they were gone.

5

Sunlight streamed in through a window.

The blue dress lay untidily over her chair.

Her head was muzzy, limbs reluctant to move from the warmth of the bed. Closing her eyes, then flicking them open again, Briony remembered the previous evening with a fresh stab of apprehension.

Jealousy.

It was a horrible emotion. It burnt between the ribs, it ate up all sensible reasoning. It made her feel . . . vulnerable. She thought of Lea, so lovely last night. Those violet eyes and the jade dress, the way she'd clung to Nick's arm. Was it their regular eating place? Exactly how much of a professional attitude did he expect from Lea, bearing in mind their relationship?

Nick's expression haunted her. It was

obvious he'd seen Matthew lean across and plant that kiss, and just as obvious that he'd drawn the wrong conclusion. Briony rested her head back on the pillow and breathed deeply, telling herself it didn't matter. Wasn't Nick having an affair with his female assistant — and trying to keep it under wraps? But as she showered and dressed she knew it did matter. It was ridiculous, but it mattered very much.

After making some fresh fruit juice and eating a light breakfast she went out of the house to find Don. His familiar shape was hunched against the wind, leaning on the fence of the paddock. Phoebe, very swollen with her pregnancy, nosed her way through late autumn grass.

Don had enough troubles of his own without being burdened. Though they were close and had always shared their problems, this time it was different. She was working for Nick because it would get Don off the hook . . . she had to see it out. It was her own fault for becoming emotionally entangled. Surely she had sense enough to realise that the feelings she had about Nick were just a residue of a silly teenage crush, something she should have come to terms with ages ago?

She heard the shouts of some of the owners with their horses. For a Sunday, the yard looked busy. Perhaps Don had finally had some luck with the fees?

Briony leaned beside him on the wooden fence. 'Not long now?' she asked, observing Phoebe's condition.

Don turned to her, making an effort to look brighter. But she knew him too well to believe the shadow of a smile. 'No,' he agreed softly, 'not long. She's in good shape, but you never really relax until it's all over.'

Briony nodded, knowing the bond between mare and owner at the time of parturition was a particularly delicate period. She had even known an owner to experience sympathetic labour when their pony was in foal. She had examined Phoebe herself and the foal was lying well for a normal delivery. Not that she could become involved, since Nick was treating her and it would be up to him to attend the birth.

'You'll be happy to hear that those people have just settled their account, thanks to you,' Don told her as Phoebe ambled towards him and nibbled his fingers.

'I only wrote a few letters.'

'You've got a business head on you, Bri. I haven't — and I might as well get used to the fact. Horses I can manage, people I'm hopeless with.'

'Then why not let Beth manage the business side? Talk it over with her?'

Don nodded, his face clouding. 'I wish I could.'

Briony smiled. 'There's nothing stopping you.'

He looked at her, shaking his head. 'There is now. I went to Beth's parents' place. Beth was out — they wouldn't tell me where. I said I'd come to collect her, and her father threatened to ring the police.'

'Don, how awful for you!'

'Then I lost my temper. I called him an unreasonable old goat and told him to get stuffed. I said Beth was my wife and if she didn't come home of her own accord I'd be back to fetch her.'

Briony couldn't help but stare in amazement. Was this really her quiet, unassuming brother who hardly ever said boo to a goose?

Don added with a deep sigh, 'He blustered for a while, went red in the face and said something about me being a loser. Then I told him to keep his nose out of my marriage — and when I'd got that off my chest, I left.' He turned back to her, his face as white as a sheet.

'Well, at least you've actually done something, Don; you just haven't stood by . . .'

Her brother shrugged. 'I suppose I enjoyed letting off steam, and I really meant what I said. I love her too much to let her go. If she screams her head off I'm still going to bring her back to where she belongs. I know I did wrong with that bet and I know I was pigheaded, but I'm never going to be such an idiot again . . . somehow I've got to persuade her I mean it.'

Briony began to worry. She felt responsible for egging him on. Just as she was going to ask him if there was a possibility of talking to Beth on neutral territory somewhere, a stable-lad called from the yard.

'I'd better start getting the place on its feet. Phoebe needs grooming and putting back into her box.'

'Leave her to me,' Briony offered, pleased at the distraction.

Phoebe was where it had all started. Something about being near the horse, feeling the warmth of the beautiful earth-brown body rubbing next to hers, sent a trail of shivers along her spine. She had no fear of Phoebe. Those huge, thickly lashed eyes were at peace today. Don had brought her on from a foal. He'd kept her as his own because normally her temperament was a stable one. In pregnancy, though, every woman was prone to change in hormonal reaction, none the less a thoroughbred mare about to foal. Briony reflected sadly that life could be a battleground for animals, with very few fighting on their side. Humans had words; animals had only action, and often those actions were misinterpreted because of human ignorance.

Phoebe gave a whinney and allowed herself to be led into her box. Briony prepared her feed, began to comb the thick dark mane, and with each stroke her thoughts wandered . . . where was Nick now? With Lea? She couldn't help but feel Lea would make it all the worse for her. And now she knew why. After last night she suspected Lea was not merely infatuated by Nick.

She was in love with him.

★   ★   ★

By Monday morning Briony had all her answers ready regarding Matthew. What she hadn't bargained for was the absence of questions. Anita explained that Nick and Ben had left in order to meet the Ministry of Agriculture officials concerning outbreaks of swine vesicular disease, and Lea was under way with open surgery. Breathing a small sigh of relief that the coast was clear, Briony undertook the morning's appointments.

As the day wore on she pondered over the probability that Saturday's encounter at Chez Françoise would be forgotten. Thank goodness the outbreak of SVD had taken up Nick's time. And when she got home that evening she had convinced herself that Nick would have dismissed the incident entirely.

The following day, just as she was treating an Alsatian for a skin infection, Anita hurried into the consulting-room.

'We've had two SOSs, Briony. Nick needs some help at Medlicott's, and Ben's got stuck in the country in a ditch. Apparently he swerved to avoid a car and went into a bog. He's going to be at least an hour or so getting towed out.'

Briony smoothed the last of the Alsatian's hind-quarter hair back into place. It was a nasty case of dermatitis, causing the animal great distress. 'I'll have to finish here, Anita, then I'll go on whichever call is the most important. Try and find out which one is, will you?'

Briony got down to clipping the surrounding hair, being careful of the lesions on the skin which were moist and painfully reddening. Cleansing the area and applying an antimicrobial cream, she finally prescribed a course of glucocorticoids to establish full recovery.

Trying not to rush through a simple set of instructions to the Alsatian's owner, she finally washed and packed her case fifteen minutes later, referring the rest of her list to Lea. Oddly enough, Lea accepted the extra workload without complaint. As she left for Ben's call, the one given priority,

Briony hoped that Lea's attitude was a good omen. Perhaps, having seen her with Matthew, Lea now felt less threatened with regard to either Nick or the work? Maybe it might even be a good idea to let her go on thinking she was romantically involved with Matthew. At least that way their relationship might improve.

Ben's call turned out to be a farmer with lame sheep. Briony examined them, discovering bacteria invading the tissue beneath the hoof horn, causing the horn to separate from the soft tissue of the feet. The foul-smelling discharge had worsened in wet conditions. Though the cases were acute they were certainly not an emergency, and she wondered, as she discussed a foot rot eradication programme with the farmer, just why Anita had isolated this as a priority case. Not that she knew what Horace Medlicott's problem was, but it was unusual for Nick to call in for help. If he had, there was no doubt he needed it.

Having settled the method of treatment, Briony reached her car just as the car-phone was ringing. Slightly out of breath, she jumped in to answer it. Her tummy turned over as Anita explained that Nick had phoned demanding to know why his SOS had been ignored.

Briony tried to think calmly. 'But what happened, Anita? I thought Ben's case took precedence?'

Anita's voice came back nervously without any constructive information. Suspecting that Anita was not divulging the whole story, she started the car and took the road to Medlicott's. Twenty minutes later she arrived at the familiar gravel path that led to his farmhouse. As she pulled on the handbrake, a grim-faced Nick strode towards her.

When he reached her, Briony knew she was in for trouble. His face was drawn and his eyes blazed.

'I'm sorry I'm late — ' she began.

'Sorry? What the hell's the good of that? I called in almost two hours ago.'

She tensed, her instincts telling her to

keep calm. She understood that he must be angry, but he must give her time to explain! 'I was the only one available to come . . . Ben got stuck as well, so I did his call first. If I'd been fully in the picture I'd have come here first.'

His face darkened, his wide shoulders taut. 'Then why didn't someone get another vet out to help me? You know we've got an arrangement with Manners on the other side of town. I had all systems go here, apart from which I looked a fool in front of the Ministry people.'

Briony shook her head, not understanding. 'I didn't think your call was so urgent. I really am sorry, but it was a complete misunderstanding.'

'It's no misunderstanding — it's sheer disorganisation, just the thing I try to avoid within the group. It's why I hired you — so there wouldn't be an infernal mess like today.'

Briony stood wordlessly, angry at his attitude, for he didn't seem to realise that her mistake wasn't deliberate. She had no answers, unfortunately. Why hadn't Anita addressed the situation? Usually she had everything under control at the surgery. Perhaps the reception staff had muddled up the calls?

'Look, I don't know how the mistake occurred, Nick. All I can say is I would have come sooner if I'd known.'

He seemed to simmer down. 'You'd better give me a hand — not that you can do anything now. The Ministry guy's gone off with a flea in his ear because there wasn't a vet available to answer all his blessed questions.'

Briony wished she could explain that it really wasn't her fault, but she knew Nick was too disturbed for the moment to discuss it rationally. And why was the Ministry man here at Medlicott's anyway? Surely there was no SVD? Sarah had looked, and acted, perfectly healthy last week.

'No . . . it's not Sarah,' Nick said, answering her thoughts. Briony kept in step as he led her towards a large sty constructed of building blocks with a corrugated iron roof. 'I hope we've caught the wretched thing in time. The permanent stock aren't affected, but Medlicott's new swine have ulcers on the feet around the coronet and between the claws.'

Briony took in her breath sharply. 'Not foot-and-mouth, surely?'

Nick unbolted the sty gate, his frown deepening. 'That's why I called in the Ministry. I was pretty certain it was another outbreak of the SVD, but the symptoms are so alike to foot-and-mouth I had to be sure.'

'And it's the SVD?'

'He's taken specimens . . . but he's ninety per cent sure it's not foot-and-mouth. Doesn't help Medlicott's pigs, though; some of them are pretty sick. I'll have to put them down.'

Briony sighed. It was bad luck for Mr Medlicott. She hoped he'd kept the new pigs separate from his resident stock. SVD wasn't usually a killer.

Outbreaks of the disease were associated with swill feeding and could be contained, but sometimes it was touch and go.

'I've a feeling some of the new breeds developed specifically to give the best meat are the most susceptible to disease,' Nick added, rubbing his chin.

'Which has happened in this case?'

'Hmm, I'm afraid so. Anyway, let's have a look in here. I've got something to show you.'

She followed Nick across the compact, freshly cleaned sty to a set of stable doors leading into a shed. When Nick urged her to duck her head and walk in she gave a gasp of delight. 'Oh, Nick, Sarah's farrowed!'

Sarah lay unusually subdued by the farrowing rail which Mr Medlicott had erected in order to stop her lying on her piglets and crushing them. The farmer had also constructed 'house of cards' bales of straw on the opposite wall where, if the sow moved, the piglets could escape into the straw. But now

136

she suckled them, their little wrinkled noses tucked deep into her belly, grunting their satisfaction.

'An hour ago her milk hadn't come down, and Medlicott was going frantic. That's why I called you in. I had to come over here and help out and leave the fellow from the Ministry chewing the end of his pencil. Needless to say, it wasn't the best of arrangements.'

'I am sorry, Nick.' Briony realised why he had been so angry. He wasn't a patient man at the best of times, and waiting for her must have seemed an eternity.

He smiled, his eyes twinkling. 'Kept me on my toes for a bit, I can tell you.'

She gave a soft laugh, watching him run his hand through the dark hair, the small flecks of grey at the temples seeming a shade more pronounced. Even the scab on his forehead was almost healed.

'What do you think of Sarah's football team?' he asked her.

Briony grinned, enjoying the sensation of standing beside him, feeling the warmth of his body. He'd every right to get angry about this afternoon, but where the fault lay she could only speculate. 'How many of them?' she asked softly, trying unsuccessfully to count the wriggling bodies.

'Ten, but I'm not sure about that little runt. Do you see him? He doesn't seem to be getting his quota.'

Briony saw with dismay a very tiny piglet trying his best to find a spare teat. But every time he nuzzled in, another stronger pair of pink feet clambered over him and squeezed him out.

'Poor little darling . . . ' She knew the chances of a casualty were high at this point. No matter what one did, whether by crushing or starving or simply by there being no great will to live, an offspring would occasionally fail to survive.

'I'll tell Medlicott to keep an eye on him,' Nick decided. 'He might have to

138

take it in and get Mrs Medlicott to feed it. Not that he'll relish the prospect. That's the way he got Sarah and Seth, and he's never had the heart to do anything but treat them like humans!'

'But to leave it . . . he wouldn't? I know he's a pig farmer and pigs usually end up as porkers, but a tiny mite like that — surely he'll try to save it?'

Nick looked down at her, a wry smile on his lips. 'I'll ask him — on your behalf.'

They watched for a while. Briony wished she had been here, not only for the farrowing, but in order to help out with the more unpleasant part of the job — the diagnosing of the SVD.

'Are you going to examine the rest of the new pigs today?'

Nick nodded. 'You'd better be on your way, hadn't you? You're on call for the next couple of nights. You'd better have a meal and grab some sleep.'

Briony smiled up at him. Her employer had a short fuse, as Anita persisted in telling her, but when the

139

explosion was over it was done and forgotten. He was careful to consider her now, remembering her duty nights. But then she had worked in more strenuous conditions than these. Grinning, she took off her anorak and walked across the sty. 'I'm going to get my overalls and I'll examine the stock with you. I need some fresh air.'

He followed her, bolting the sty door behind him. When he looked up his expression was rueful. 'Are you sure you're not biting off just a bit more than you can chew?'

'I've got a healthy appetite . . . ' The words tumbled out before she could think what she was saying. The natural progression to appetite was food . . . and to food, Chez Françoise. She watched his brows meet and guessed at his next remark.

'Talking of appetites, I trust you enjoyed yourself?'

Briony began to walk quickly to her car for the change of overalls. She didn't particularly want a postmortem over Matthew, especially now. 'If you're referring to Saturday — I did, thank you.'

He was beside her, unwilling to let the subject drop. 'Lea's observation was pretty astute, I thought. You made a handsome couple. Prior was almost eating you in preference to the cuisine.'

Briony swivelled on her heel as she reached the car, her cheeks fanning scarlet. 'I didn't think I was being watched to that extent.'

'I could hardly avoid watching! Everyone else in the restaurant was.'

'That's ridiculous!'

Leaning his arm beside her on to the roof of the car, his other stretching out to open the door, pinning her to the spot, Nick growled, 'Do you know what you're getting yourself into? Can't you see what's going on? You tell me he's a friend — and a friend of your father's. You also tell me he's never made a pass . . . or have I misunderstood again? Don't you think it's a little strange that he should start showing an interest just as you begin working for me?'

'I don't think I'll bother even answering that,' she retorted, her back level to the car, unable to move sideways.

'I'll take it I'm right, in that case. You and he aren't having an affair?'

'How dare you be so personal?'

'I dare because I care about a good locum I've just managed to get, finding herself distracted from her work by an idiot like Prior.'

'Matthew's not an idiot!'

'No . . . you're probably right there. He's shrewd enough to know you're back in Bagbourne and fair game. I wouldn't mind betting your father's well aware of every move he's making.'

Briony's blue eyes turned to ice as she felt her heart beat angrily under her ribs. 'And just how much do you think you know about my father's intentions?'

The smile that twisted his lips made her legs turn to water, for she had the feeling he was about to tell her. Slowly he eased himself away, his eyes mocking. 'I've got the best source of information — you, Briony. Remember? You didn't seem to have any objection to telling me your life story. Besides which, have you forgotten we virtually grew up on each other's doorsteps? I know just how much your father hated losing his family — about as much as my father hated losing his. They were stubborn men, and I can see by the way you're looking at me that you're just as stubborn as your father ever was. Too stubborn to see that Prior will have you exactly where he wants you — tied to his apron strings — before you can say Jack Robinson.'

Enough was enough! She wasn't going to be told what to do with her life! Perhaps she had been wrong to think Nick didn't bear a grudge about the past. Perhaps he cared far more than she suspected and through spite he was trying to blacken Matthew's name. Well, she wouldn't have it!

'What makes you think I wouldn't jump at the opportunity of being . . .

tied to his apron strings, as you call it?'
She glared at him, her pulse accelerating. 'He might be exactly the type of
person I'd choose to spend my life with.
I don't see you having any reservations
about Lea. And I think it's fair enough
to make comparisons in this case by the
way she was hanging on to you on
Saturday night.' She eased herself
upright. 'Now, if you'll excuse me while
I put on my overalls, I think it's time we
both got down to looking at your
client's stock . . . don't you?'

* * *

It wasn't going to work . . . it just
wasn't.

Today underlined for Briony what
common sense had already told her
from the start. One risked too much
when mixing personal and professional
relationships, even when the circumstances were clear-cut.

She soaked in the bath she had run,
hoping the phone wouldn't ring for a

call out. If it did, fresh clothes were lying on her bed, her case and keys downstairs by the front door.

The supper she'd shared with Don when she'd arrived back from Medlicott's at half-past eight had been like the Last Supper! Lost in their own thoughts, they had tactfully skirted their respective problems.

Beth hadn't called.

Nick and the SVD outbreak was an even trickier subject. To say Nick hadn't spoken a word to her for the past three hours as they had inspected the pigs wasn't an understatement. It had been a relief to get home, to shake off the tension and slip into the hot, foamy water.

She didn't belong in Nick Lloyd's world. To try to go back in time was a big mistake, she thought miserably as she soaped her long legs, hot from being under the overalls for hours. And wasn't that what she'd been doing — recalling a Nick Lloyd who was obviously dead, a figment of her imagination from the past?

She had worked hard to serve her apprenticeship, her training was over . . . done with! Skirmishes like this afternoon with Nick and the hassle with Lea only highlighted the impossibility of the situation. As for Don . . . he was a fully grown man. He had been working well up until now with Nick — he should really be sorting out his finances or he might never learn the valuable lesson the circumstances afforded.

Besides, there was something going on deep inside her that she didn't fully understand. It wasn't tangible, nothing she could practically fight.

The feelings she had for Nick were far too dangerous. There couldn't possibly be a future in either a professional or personal relationship. She didn't want to end up with a broken heart, nor did she want to give Lea a chance to poison Nick's mind against her. And Matthew? Well, he wasn't really an issue, though Nick seemed to think he would affect her work. For Nick to be concerned so obviously for his own ends made her angry. She was a woman first and foremost — and vulnerable. And in Nick's mind she seemed to be neither. She was a business asset, a bridging loan without the interest.

There was only one real solution. She'd have to talk to Don, break the news to him first. He would understand.

Then Nick. She would work through November if she was forced to . . . until he found another locum. Then she would get right away, perhaps even further south. It would mean taking on another locum's position until Don paid her back.

But at least this time her head would rule her heart.

6

It was bitterly cold.

A searing wind drove Briony across the car park to the surgery. She pulled up the collar of her coat, shivering in anticipation.

She would do it immediately. If she waited, she would put it off forever or muddle up the short, decisive little speech announcing her resignation. Rehearsing again the sentences she had sat up half the night preparing, she almost fell over Lea crouched in the hallway. 'This dog's had a fit! I've given him an injection . . . can you get on with open surgery?' Lea asked without saying good morning.

Briony surveyed the dog, whom they had not quite managed to get into a consulting-room. The line of anxious human faces in Reception peered out to see what was happening. To add to the confusion Ben caught her arm as he flew past.

'Briony, thank heavens! I have to dash . . . an emergency at one of our studs. Could you possibly take my appointments?' He thrust a crumpled piece of paper into her hand. 'You're an angel! Details are all in there!'

She stared at the note, scrawled and illegible. By the time she looked up he had gone and Lorraine had replaced him.

'First one's in a bit of a state — a spaniel who got stuck in a rainwater butt overnight. Can you see him now?'

Briony nodded. 'OK, but remember to fit in Ben's, will you, as we go along? Is Anita in yet?'

'No, it's her day off. And there's worse to come. Nick's not here either.'

So there was no chance of talking to Anita about the confusion at Medlicott's yesterday. Not that it mattered now. If she wasn't going to be here for very much longer perhaps it was best not to start cross-questioning anyone.

She didn't want to leave with bad feeling. She smiled, resigned, at Lorraine. 'I suppose Nick's on a call out?'

Lorraine looked back to the noisy waiting-room, eager to go. 'No. He's had to go to Scotland — of all places! Doesn't his father live in some remote castle on the west coast? Lea's got all the details . . . she told me he was flying back home tomorrow, so there won't be too much chaos, I hope.'

Lorraine's words rang in Briony's ears as she hurried along to her consulting-room. Nick in Scotland! Well, that put paid to any plans of her own — for the time being. All that thinking into the small hours . . .

Resolving that she'd put the whole matter out of her mind, she attended to the spaniel's difficulties, which were mostly shock and drenched nostrils. A succession of animal woes followed — lacerations and bruises, minor cuts and abrasions, a particularly nasty abscess and a viral infection. By the time Reception was empty she realised the clock had edged to around one. Her tummy rumbled ominously.

'Phone for you, Briony,' Lorraine called. 'I've switched it through to the office.'

She was astonished to hear Beth's voice. 'Beth! How lovely. Where are you?'

'Bagbourne. Can you meet me for lunch? It's really very important, or I wouldn't ask.'

Rather impulsively Briony suggested a coffee-house.

'Perfect,' Beth agreed quickly. 'Meet you there in fifteen minutes.'

Wondering what crisis was next on the agenda, Briony drove into Bagbourne, wishing fervently that she had rung Don. As if there weren't enough complications in her life without getting mixed up between these two!

Beth waved, her mane of chocolate-brown hair distinct among the other heads in the coffee-house, her soft green eyes welcoming as she saw Briony. 'Did I drag you away from anything special?'

Sitting opposite her, Briony shook her head and smiled. 'Nothing that can't wait. Have you ordered?'

'Just coffees.' The pretty face was bereft of make-up and looking distinctly pale — a reflection of Don's exactly.

'It's good to see you, Beth . . . only I do wish you'd phoned Don, not me. He's the one you should be talking to.'

Beth nodded. 'I just had to talk to someone. You see, it's my parents. They want me to have a trial separation — just for a while, to give myself time.'

'Oh, Beth, do you really think that will help?'

The coffee arrived and it was a few moments before Beth spoke again. 'I thought perhaps I could ask you about . . . how Don really feels?'

'He loves you Beth, desperately. You must know that. This whole thing's been blown out of proportion. I know you two could make it work if you really tried.'

The green eyes glittered, announcing

a small, glossy tear. 'I miss him, Briony. What's so awful is ... we've been trying for such a long time to have a family, and it's been useless — until now, of all times. I'm pregnant, you see. I got it confirmed this morning.'

'Oh, Beth, that's not awful, it's marvellous!'

Beth pulled a handkerchief from a voluminous bag and dabbed at her nose. 'But I'm so worried about our debts. They seem to be hanging over our head like the sword of Damocles. Especially the feed merchant and Nick's bill. How are we ever going to pay them? With a baby coming it'll only make matters far worse.'

Briony groaned inwardly. A financial crisis would indeed catapult Beth back into her parents' corner. She had to try to allay some of Beth's fears, for her brother's sake. 'Listen, the owners are gradually settling their bills — and Don has paid the feed merchant. Things are really looking very much brighter.'

'But there's still Nick Lloyd — and

he's the most important one.'

Briony sipped nervously at her coffee. What was she to do? Beth's news had shed a completely different light on matters. A baby! How could she possibly think of opting out of helping Don now? Well, she couldn't. She had to stick by them even if it meant continuing at the surgery.

'You don't have to worry about Nick either,' Briony told her. 'As a matter of fact, we've come to an arrangement. Nick won't press Don, not until he's ready.'

Beth drew an audible breath, frowning. 'Really? But I don't understand . . .'

As she leaned across to reassure Beth's small fidgeting fingers Briony's coat tipped a teaspoon to the floor. A man bent down to pick it up, returning it to her with a smile.

'Dr Westerley!' She would never forget that face. Colour flooded her cheeks.

'I'm sorry . . . do I know you?'

'I was at the hospital on the night you treated a friend of mine.'

'How rude of me not to remember. And I'm sure I wouldn't forget such a beautiful smile. Who is our mutual friend?'

'Oh . . . ' Briony hesitated, feeling cross with herself. Now she would get involved in the subject she was trying so hard to forget. 'Nick . . . Nicholas Lloyd?'

'Of course! And you're the young lady with copper-coloured hair — his new locum. He told me all about you when I fixed up that wound of his.'

'Did he?' Briony looked at Beth, who was listening avidly, her eyebrows raised.

'You acted with great presence of mind, Miss — er — '

'Beaumont . . . Briony Beaumont.'

The doctor's grin widened as he added, 'Frankly, I think you're just what the doctor ordered as far as Nick goes — if you'll excuse the pun. After that miserable episode with Samantha

— but enough said. I have to rush . . . I'm late on duty as it is. It's been good to meet you, Briony. Remember me to Nick, will you?'

He nodded to Beth, who sat with her eyes almost popping out of their sockets. She said quickly as she watched the disappearing figure, 'Wow! If Nick discussed the colour of your hair with him — what else did he discuss?'

'Oh, rubbish!'

'Nick was obviously impressed with you — and that's a wonder, considering his opinion of women — I mean, after Samantha Forbes dropped out of the picture so quickly . . . '

Who was Samantha Forbes? Briony waited for enlightenment, and received none. Beth chatted deliriously about babies, her worries over money seemingly allayed as they strolled together into the car park.

Briony asked, 'Are you sure you don't mind me staying until I find a flat?'

Beth giggled, her cheeks beginning to glow. 'You don't think I'm going to go through all that morning sickness without someone to complain to, do you? Because Don will be too busy with his beloved horses to notice how I feel. If I were a mare in foal it would be another story!'

Briony drove back to work. Last night her own problems had seemed overwhelming, and she'd decided Don would have to find the solution to his without her help. But now he was reunited with a pregnant — and happy — wife, leaving the practice was out of the question, at least for the time being.

*　★　★*

The afternoon was quieter. As Lorraine bore in a welcome cup of tea just before closing, Briony plucked up enough courage to ask the question which had been buzzing in her mind since lunchtime. 'I wonder . . . does the name Samantha Forbes ring a bell, Lorraine?'

'Samantha? Why, yes. She was locum for us several years ago, about the time

Nick had his brother Luke to stay from Canada, I think.'

Briony nodded, feeling guilty, as though she were prising some terrible secret out. 'Do you know what — er — happened to her?'

Lorraine blinked, her brown eyes widening in the effort to recollect. 'Well ... I'm not sure, actually. Samantha was the sort of person who liked to do things her own way — not that Nick and Jack minded. But when Lea started here there was friction. Samantha left, just before she was due to get married.'

'Because she was giving up work?'

Lorraine frowned. 'No, I don't think so. Not in that sense. All I can tell you is that Nick came in one morning and said she'd left the practice. I never saw her again.'

Briony's eyebrows knitted as she tried to piece together the fragments of information. 'He was upset at being let down, I suppose.'

Lorraine nodded. 'In more ways than

one. It was Nick she was engaged to, you see.'

Briony felt colour visibly drain from her face. 'I . . . I had no idea!'

'Surprised?'

'Very. I never imagined Nick as the marrying type . . . not at all.'

When she was alone, Briony sat down at her desk. The thoughts in her mind jostled for space. Nick, engaged? Hardly believable. She'd imagined him as the stereotype bachelor with women as a kind of second string to his professional bow. The fact that he hadn't admitted to an affair with Lea only confirmed her suspicions. She could understand Lea's dislike of her now. Lea had managed to dispatch Samantha, only to be faced with the prospect of yet another female on the scene!

* * *

Briony awoke with a jump. Was it a dream, the sound of Don's voice?

As she threw back the covers and tried to blink the sleep from her eyes, Don's face appeared, ghastly white around the door. 'Briony!'

'Who . . . is that you, Don?'

Her brother opened the door wider, his face just a misty patch in the gloom of her bedroom. Was it still night or early morning . . . or had she overslept?

'It's Phoebe — she's started labour. Can you come? I know it's an ungodly hour . . . '

'Give me ten minutes,' she mumbled, coming awake. Ferreting blindly around the room after her brother had gone, she slid on warm cords and a thick jumper. She brushed her teeth, splashed cold water over her face, which did the trick, and then pulled back her mop of hair into a band.

As she bolted downstairs, the last twenty-four hours ran like a video through her mind. Nick had returned. His flight had been late and he'd arrived in a flurry of missed appointments. They had hardly talked . . . he'd looked tired, exhaustion carving deep lines in his cheeks. But his eyes had held hers briefly in a small oasis of calm after the last client had gone from surgery.

And now Phoebe, recalcitrant all day yesterday, had begun labour. Had Don been with her throughout the night?

Downstairs, Beth, in her dressing-gown, was making coffee. It was reassuring to see her small figure moving about the kitchen again. The house had seemed disastrously empty without her. 'Here . . . have some before you go; you're going to need it.' She filled a mug, the china hot between Briony's fingers.

'Is it really five?' Briony asked, glancing at her wristwatch.

'I'm afraid so. Don's been up since two. Phoebe isn't taking very kindly to labour pains.'

'Have you called Nick?'

'Don's just done it. He's as nervous as a kitten. You'd think he was having a baby himself.'

Though Beth made light of it, Briony glimpsed apprehension in the green eyes. 'A lot of people's hopes are riding on Phoebe, aren't they?' she murmured softly.

Briony smiled. 'To a certain extent. But there really isn't any need for you to worry. She's strong and healthy and tough! A Beaumont down to the ground.'

Beth laughed, but her eyes were still uneasy.

'Why don't you go back to bed?' Briony suggested as she threw on her anorak. 'And I'll get Don to come back to the house.'

As she hurried across the yard to Phoebe's box, there was tense excitement in the air, the sort of excitement that was contagious. The crescent moon edged its way behind a last stray cloud. A few remaining stars twinkled in the dusky sky of dawn. It was a fine November morning . . . and Briony's heart was jumping around like a frightened deer. Phoebe would sail through her delivery; she had already borne a previous foal, there should be no complications . . .

A crack of golden light shone from the stable. She peeled open the door and saw her brother. 'Thanks for coming.' His voice was thin and his lips twitched. Phoebe moved restlessly, her head flying up and down, that wild look in her eyes.

'I can't seem to settle her.' Don gathered the rope and made another attempt to control the mare, but she shook him off, turning full circle, her neck strained in protest.

'It's because you're worrying. She knows. You're too close, Don. Go in to Beth; I'll wait for Nick.' She took hold of the rope, led Phoebe around the box, then tethered her. 'Go on, Don. You're only making things worse.'

She watched the gloomy disappearance of her brother with wry amusement. Beth was right; the last place for him was here.

A while later, she heard a footfall she

recognised, and with a lurch of her heart she turned to see Nick push open the stable door.

'Hello!' He smiled. The dark eyes, fresh from sleep, sparkled.

'Don's gone in,' she said, all at once thinking she ought to explain her presence here, for Phoebe was not her patient. 'He wouldn't be much help, I'm afraid. As Beth says, it's almost as though he's going through the birth himself.'

'That's understandable.' Nick put down his case and stripped off his coat. 'I'll guess we'll manage.' Did the 'we' indicate that he was counting on her staying? 'How is she doing?'

'She has some milk ejection reflex — and the vulva's lengthening, with a slight puffiness of the vulva lips. I don't think she'll be long.'

'What about the foal? How's he lying?'

'The forelegs and muzzle are against the cervix. What I am concerned about, though, is a previous vulva operation.'

He nodded, standing beside her to examine Phoebe. 'You're right. I think I'm going to have to snip her. And this time I shall make sure she doesn't have the energy to object!'

Briony watched him give the injection, and in silence they waited for Phoebe's reaction.

'I'd rather have her lying down. Do you think you could persuade her? Perhaps she'll be more responsive to another female.' Nick was obviously well aware of the practical considerations. After his experience with Phoebe in the yard, he wasn't going to take any chances.

'I'll try.' It seemed a long while before she was able to move in closely. Untethering her and grasping the head-collar, she rubbed gentle fingers behind a nervous ear. Soon Phoebe went down, the weight of her collapsing sending thousands of dust mites into the air.

Briony knelt too. 'I'll try to keep her off her feet — though I don't promise any more rugby tackles from this angle if she decides to get up.'

Nick grinned as he too knelt, his long legs tucked under him. Briony felt an unexpected surge of warmth fill her body as she saw him gently slide his large hands over the sweating brown body.

The small operation completed, two accurate strokes made without fuss, Phoebe didn't even raise her head. Briony watched him as he worked. Confident, assured, efficient, he had scarcely begun before he had finished. She suddenly had the feeling she was riding a merry-go-round, her tummy reeling in all directions. The phenomenon, she told herself firmly, was not because she was in his presence and affected by some primitive energy reaching her, but more likely her concern for the animal, the early hour — and no breakfast.

'Two feet . . . one muzzle . . . ' Nick said, catching her glance. Quickly she looked away back to Phoebe, trying to control the alarming physical manifestations running through her body. This was the moment of birth! What was she doing, behaving like an impressionable sixteen-year-old? Delivery needed to be completed as quickly as possible so as to avoid pressure on the umbilical cord.

'Come beside me,' he said, mild amusement in his voice. 'Phoebe's calm enough now.'

With legs that didn't feel at all her own Briony managed to do as he said. She felt Phoebe jerk in a powerful contraction. Nick's attention slipped back to the delivery, and as he gave gentle guidance, with his strong, patient fingers delivering one foreleg in advance of the other, the bulk of the foal's elbows passed safely through the pelvic outlet.

'Phoebe has a son,' Nick murmured, glancing at her.

Briony was assailed with a compelling tenderness. Her hands went out to support the new foal, covered in its moist silken web. 'He's breathing perfectly,' she whispered, placing her hand gently on the left side of the chest over the heart just behind the elbows. Checking her wristwatch, she counted. 'Seventy per minute.'

The foal turned on his brisket, withdrawing his hind legs from the vagina. 'He's beautifully healthy,' Nick said with unmistakable pride. Briony watched him deal with the afterbirth, tying the amnion to the cord as it passed from the mare, his large hands accomplishing delicate movements with graceful ease.

Later, Briony dressed the stump of the foal's navel. Utter satisfaction overwhelmed her. Working with Nick was no effort; they seemed to have a perfect rapport. She knew it wasn't the same for many professionals; there were often clashes which were irreconcilable. She'd rather feared it might be like that with Nick. They'd had more downs than ups to begin with, but instinct told her quite differently now. Their partnership was fluid and natural.

'Time for us to let nature take over,'

Nick whispered, touching her elbow.

She nodded, getting to her feet. The bonding of mare to foal would take place through a combination of sight and smell. Phoebe would taste her amniotic fluid in the foal's saturated coat, fixing her son's identity in her brain.

Nick stood upright, his clothing littered with bits of straw. Looking down from his tall height, he grinned at her. 'He should stand soon. Let's move to the back where we can watch without disturbing them.'

They went quietly to the corner of the stable, easing down in the straw. His body was warm next to hers. She could feel that restless energy pulsating, acting like electricity. She caught her breath in her throat as he settled himself, his arm, because of the small confines, sneaking around her back.

'The foal's unsteady, but he senses the milk,' Nick whispered. 'I hope he — '

Phoebe clambered to her feet.

Briony gasped, and both of them tensed as her straining body moved within inches of the foal.

'There's nothing we can do,' Nick murmured, squeezing her shoulder, 'except sit tight and hope for the best while he's getting his bearings.' His breath was on her cheek, for somehow she seemed to be leaning against the hard wall of his chest. 'You want to move him out of harm's way, don't you?' he muttered in her ear.

Briony nodded, feeling the heaviness of his arm as it encircled her. Was he aware of his action, or was he too absorbed in Phoebe to know what he was doing?

'You know what you look like?' he asked suddenly, looking down at her, and with his free hand he reached across to remove pieces of straw from her hair.

'Awful at the moment, I should think.'

He shook his head. 'No. Quite the opposite. Very beautiful, very natural.'

He lifted a long strand of coppery hair and laid it gently down on her shoulder. 'I'm glad of the opportunity to speak to you. I haven't had much chance since I arrived back from Scotland. About that mix-up at Medlicott's — Lea gave the details to Anita and they got confused somehow. Probably because there was such a rush at the practice with the farm work at the same time. Sorry I bit your head off.' Then his hand began to move down her arm, massaging her skin into life.

'I . . . I suppose it couldn't be helped,' Briony stammered, a little voice inside shrieking that it was unfair and that a contrivance had gone on somewhere along the line, and she had a pretty good idea who had contrived it! But Nick's expression, the touch of his fingers, the love-like pain that caught at her throat as she looked at him, diminished any sense of bitterness. She put it out of her mind . . . which wasn't difficult at a moment like this.

She could feel the solid throbbing of her heart as his lips turned up in wry amusement. 'I'm not terribly good at apologies, I'm afraid,' he told her.

In the back of her brain she heard Phoebe making small chattering noises as she ground her teeth. It was a safe and familiar sound, and it meant she was still part of the real world, that she wasn't drowning in fantasy.

But the picture of Lea came back into her mind. And the question posed itself — how many times had Nick Lloyd turned situations conveniently in his own direction as far as women were concerned? She had the overwhelming feeling that she was just about to find out and not be able to do a thing about it as he tipped her chin towards him. Weakly she allowed him to do it.

As he kissed her slowly, she was silenced. She laid her hands momentarily against his chest, in token protest. No, she thought frantically, this can't be happening again. I don't want it to happen! But as his mouth stirred hers into life, her lids closed, her body gave way to his. Suddenly, ferociously, he possessed her, her own hands travelling treacherously across the straining material of his shirt. The hard muscles beneath his skin moved sensuously under her touch.

His smell intoxicated her. There was no cosmetic odour this time, just the smell of inexhaustible masculinity. She heard his muffled laughter as his hands ran up under her sweater, exploring the skin beneath so that she stiffened at first. Then as he kissed the soft warm skin under her chin and along the curve of her cheek she gave up her struggle. One part of her yearned for more, the other was shouting that there was only one conclusion to a situation like this. How persuasive he was, how intolerably exciting, how much she wanted him — and yet what could come of it? Torn between her surging desire and fresh waves of doubt, she trembled uncontrollably.

'What's the matter?' Nick's voice was

husky as she tried to draw away.

'Nothing,' she lied, her muscles tensing.

'A few seconds ago you were enjoying yourself. Now you're as stiff as a poker. What have I done wrong?'

'You haven't done anything,' she told him, her limbs actively trembling. 'At least, you haven't done anything yet, Nick . . . and that's the way I intend it to stay. I really think I'd better go — '

His hands tightened on her, keeping her where she was. 'What are you running away from, Briony?'

'I'm not running from anything — or anyone! I just don't believe in mixing business and pleasure — and I didn't think you did either.'

'You were happy to mix it a few seconds ago . . . unless I'm very much mistaken. Don't you think you owe yourself a moment or two of relaxation?'

That comment hurt. Her cheeks stung and she pulled sharply away, getting shakily to her feet. She tried to keep her voice low. Having an altercation in here was the last thing she wanted. 'You asked me once,' she began slowly, 'to bear in mind that you wanted a professional attitude at all times. But when it suits you, you choose to disregard your own stipulations. Or am I mistaken, Nick? Is there one rule for a man, another for a woman?'

He rose, his large body dwarfing her. His expression of mild amusement annoyed her. She wouldn't be treated like a plaything, nor would she assume the same sort of role as Lea or Samantha. She was, in all truth, desperately attracted to him. He stirred a feverish, almost archaic desire in her that she had never felt before. And perhaps he was right; perhaps she was too frightened to face it. Yet what was the point in all this? Nick's attitude to life was egotistical, full of pure male arrogance. She hated that. And it seemed he deceived quite easily — first Samantha, now Lea. And they were only two women she knew of!

'It's an interesting theory . . . the dominant role as opposed to the subservient one.' He tipped his head calmly to one side. 'Perhaps we ought to discuss it a little more fully. The theme is obviously close to your heart. But then I should know that, shouldn't I? It tallies with your ideal of avoiding feelings at all costs lest you fail in your ambition to achieve complete independence.'

'I've never said that!'

'As near as damn it. This . . . relationship . . . you're expecting to fall neatly into its pigeonhole after you've gained ultimate success career-wise — does it include falling in love, or do you propose to steer clear of that particular pitfall in life?'

Briony swallowed hard. Now he was provoking her — and enjoying it! She moved to go past him, but he barred her way. 'Let me pass, please.'

'Only if you agree that this is . . . merely a postponement.'

She stared up at him, narrowing her

blue eyes. 'Postponement of what?'

'Getting to know one another better. You've got to admit we've made a damn good start this morning.'

She pushed past him, and to her relief he let her go. She glanced back momentarily, as she reached the stable door. He was leaning, his broad, muscular forearms interlocked across his chest, against the wall. She could barely see his eyes in the shadows, but she knew their ironic expression well enough.

'You're missing the best — as usual,' he told her, his voice amused. 'The foal is beginning to suckle.'

7

Beth opened the jar of pickled onions, sniffing. 'I could eat the lot,' she sighed longingly, sitting down at the breakfast table.

Don scooped up his empty plate and bent to kiss the top of his wife's head. 'We're going to have a son — it's got to be.'

'Just because I've got a craving for onions?' Beth retaliated, looking up with mischievous green eyes.

'Just because you've got a craving for onions and piccalilli and curry!'

Briony listened to them, lowering dishes into the soapy water, smiling to herself. They didn't seem to mind — even notice her presence about the place. Babies, or the promise of them, seemed to make an extraordinary difference to the atmosphere of a house.

Already cuddly fur toys and strings of

beads adorned the nursery, a room which had waited so long for an occupant. And with Beth's announcement had come a new Don, drawing back his shoulders, lifting his chin. He was reading books on babies, baby rearing, talking to babies.

Even Phoebe's foal, Apollo, took second place. A week old, he was satin-grey and long-legged. Normally Don would have wasted hour upon hour over him, simply drooling. But now Beth was complaining that her husband was continually under her feet, a symptom of pregnancy she hadn't bargained for!

Was this what marriage was about? wondered Briony as she turned to collect the last remnants of breakfast from the table. If it was, then in Beth's eyes this morning there was a glow any woman would covet.

'Bye, Sis.' Don was beside her, smiling. 'For goodness' sake hide those onions from her, will you?' he whispered with a wicked gleam.

'I wouldn't dare!'

'How's Nick?' Beth asked, a little too eagerly, when they were alone. Briony felt her sister-in-law's gaze burn her shoulder-blades. Nick seemed to be flavour of the month at the moment after the coffee-house incident. And with little else to do for most of the day Beth had ascribed a liberal amount of time in gathering from the grapevine a harvest of belated gossip.

'If you mean how is Nick in a personal sense, I wouldn't know. You'd have to ask Lea Hughes for the answer to that question.'

'Meaning?'

Briony heard the sharp crunch of an onion and turned to see Beth chewing.

'Meaning Nick and I share a purely professional relationship and — '

'OK, I can take a hint.' And, not taking the hint at all, Beth continued, 'It's just that I can't remotely imagine he's attracted to Lea Hughes. She came out here once — and, to be perfectly honest, she didn't have the time of day for us. I can't see Nick falling for someone with zilch personality.'

'Well . . . ' Briony sighed, returning her attention to the wet dishes ' . . . he does, and there's an end to it. It's none of my business, anyway.'

'If you want to know what I think,' Beth persevered, 'I think you're suspicious of him still, and it's down to all that silly trouble the two families had when you and Don were children. Which is, I have to say, typical of a woman. I mean, not wanting to get involved again with a dominant male. At least, you sort of do, but you don't — if you see what I mean.'

Briony's eyes widened, her full mouth dropping open in astonishment. 'And whose theory is that . . . Dr Spock's?'

'I am getting rather good, aren't I?' Beth grinned smugly. 'It's all these books on kids Don's reading into the small hours. Reading aloud, may I add!'

'Well, as far as our childhood was concerned — '

'Saying is one thing, apparently, and believing is another. It's what you think unconsciously that counts. I wouldn't mind betting that deep down you fancy Nick Lloyd like mad!'

Briony promptly closed her mouth, wishing she weren't prone to blushing. 'I'll excuse you from saying such a daft thing because you're pregnant,' she muttered, trying to change the subject by resorting to the lowest form of bribery possible — handing her sister-in-law the new jar of sweet pickle.

Beth accepted it greedily. 'As I was saying . . . it's different for men. Their emotions don't get in the way so much. Ours do.'

'I'm not emotionally involved!'

'Aren't you? Well, why are you getting so het up, then? But of course, you don't want to know what I think, so I'll just shut up.' A grin spread over Beth's face. 'I think I'll make chilli tonight with some homemade chutney. Thanks for the pickle.'

Very grateful that the topic had lost

out to food, Briony was at last released to drive to work. Beth couldn't be further from the truth. If the past still held any hold over her, by now she would be embroiled in a raging affair with Nick, but over the last few days she had regained her perspective . . . nevertheless, against her will, the thought of the touch of his hands on her body made her head swim and she almost swerved into the middle of the road.

Had she ever really stopped loving him — or at least the idea of him? Why had she never gone further than a superficial relationship with another man and drowned herself in work instead? Because, if she was honest, she compared every other man in her life to the rosy, dream-lover image of Nicholas Lloyd. Dreams were larger than life, eternally sweet. And mortal men fell short of fantasies.

Now she had satisfied herself on that score, banishing the disturbing images she had of him from her mind, she tried to concentrate on her work schedule. Ripples of uncertainty flowed through the farming community — and that was what she should be occupied with, not Nick's caresses.

The SVD had worried the farmers, though indeed the outbreak had been contained. She'd had to help Nick and Ben on calls, many of them taking up hours that weren't designated as working time. The increased momentum had been immensely tiring, but at least it had kept them all at a healthy distance. She was also worried about Medlicott's tiny pig, not ten days old and struggling for life. It was on this matter that her mind dwelt as she walked into the office.

A face displaying an irritable tiredness and eyes embroidered with tiny lines became visible behind the *Veterinary Record*. 'Morning,' came Nick's solemn greeting.

'You've had a disturbed night,' Briony ventured, feeling the tension ooze.

'Hmm. Two calls, one at three, the other at five — a Caesar and a horse with ragwort poisoning. The Caesar was OK, but the horse wasn't. I'm afraid it resulted in a disappointing outcome.'

'Did you get any sleep at all?'

'A couple of hours.'

She said quickly, 'At least you can relax tomorrow. I'm on call for the next few days.'

Nick nodded, a gleam in his eye. 'Prior won't like that, will he? I mean, your job eating into your social time. I expect he's been quite put out with all the extra work you've put in.'

Why was it that when she argued with Nick she felt she had lost from the very outset? 'Matthew has no bearing on my job. My work comes first and foremost, and you know that. If you didn't, you wouldn't be employing me.'

He raised thick black, doubtful eyebrows. 'By the way he monopolises your lunch-hours I would have thought he was having a good go at initiating a change of mind regarding your working here.'

Briony frowned, trying to think what he meant. Then it clicked. Yesterday she had gone for sandwiches in town. Unable to resist the bookshop, she'd popped in briefly, bumping into Matthew, who was buying papers.

'Business in Salisbury?' she'd asked, surprised to see him.

'No, I came to see you, actually. I've got two theatre tickets burning a hole in my pocket. How do you fancy a mad weekend away from all this?'

The tickets were for *Phantom of the Opera*. But she hadn't been tempted. Somehow she didn't think a weekend away with him was meant in the context he wanted her to believe. 'I'd love it, Matthew, but we're desperate at work,' she excused not untruthfully. 'I'm afraid I couldn't spare a weekend at the moment.'

His disappointment was obvious, but he'd taken it well enough. The friendly arm he had thrown around her had taken perhaps just a little longer than she would have liked to wriggle free from.

'I was in the bookshop to . . . I didn't want to break up the happy party,' Nick muttered, his tanned forehead pleated. He probably thought she was in fact wasting time yesterday in view of the fact that they were rushed off their feet at work, plus the fact that Matthew really did appear to get under his skin.

'Are you always so churlish after broken nights?' Briony asked with rueful humour. 'I'd hate to catch you on a bad day.'

The dark eyes, complete with greyish rings, absorbed her rebuke. 'Point taken. I'll mind my own business. It's no excuse, I know, but utter lack of sleep doesn't agree with me.'

She nodded, liking the way his eyes changed so rapidly into warm, dark pools of browny gold. 'You've been flat out this week. Can't you grab a few hours today?'

He shrugged. 'No time. I'm meeting

the Ministry chap at ten . . . the one I had the upset with at Medlicott's. I can't afford to do the same thing again. Then I've got a couple more calls . . . not terribly important, but I'll have to make them all the same.'

Briony gathered her things together. 'Can I help? I'm finished here at one.'

A smile danced under the smoky blue stubble of his beard. 'That's very magnanimous of you.'

'It is, isn't it? Put it down to a soft heart.'

'After last week I thought you'd be sticking strictly to the rules to teach me a lesson.'

'I had considered it.' She laughed softly.

'In fact,' he said slowly, 'I was wondering if you'd been avoiding me for that reason.'

Still with amusement on her lips, she shook her head. 'And I was thinking much the same of you.'

For a moment he held her glance, and then they laughed. He got up from his desk, stretching his long legs, casually ambling towards her. The laughter etched handsome lines at the corners of his mouth as he drew close. 'You don't know what you've let yourself in for, offering to help out. One's a yearling for stitching, the other's a lame pony. I haven't the remotest idea what that's all about.'

Briony was soon to discover. Opting for visiting the rather aged roan who had been exposed to an over-consumption of lush grass, she took the best part of an hour to convince her novice owners that this was the cause. She administered an injection of phenylbutazone and advised a diet of hay and water while the laminitis was at its peak. Recommending that the pony be bedded on peat to provide some support to the sole, she still had reservations that her diagnosis had not been fully comprehended. The family had newly acquired the pony, which had seemed a bargain at its low price. Telling the teenager and her parents they had to cope with a tough regime of treatment wasn't easy. But finally, reasonably confident that they would ascribe to it, she turned her car on to the road as an easterly wind began to blow the tops of the trees.

Travelling back to the surgery, she wondered what she might do with the remainder of the afternoon. She didn't feel like going back home. It was a glorious day, fresh and dry with intermittent clouds rolling across a blue sky. Her thoughts turned to Mr Medlicott and his litter of pigs. It was on the way. Perhaps she should just look in? Convincing herself that she had the nine healthy piglets' welfare at heart, she drove into Medlicott's yard, looking forward mainly to seeing one in particular.

Mr Medlicott, minus the formidable Sarah, walked, shovel in hand, to greet her.

'You heard about my new pigs?' His brows met in the middle of his forehead.

'Yes. I'm very sorry about the SVD, Mr Medlicott. But thank goodness all the others are well, Sarah and Seth too. Nick said there was no more trouble with Sarah's milk.'

'She's as bright as a button. Can't say the same for the little 'un, though. 'Spect you've come to see him, haven't you?'

Briony grinned shyly. She could hide nothing from the farmer. 'You're right, Mr Medlicott, this isn't really an official call. I was just passing and I couldn't help but wonder how he was. Has Mrs Medlicott managed the feeds?'

The big man looked doubtful. 'Dunno where she gets the energy! You'd better come and see him for yourself.'

On the way to the house, Briony enquired about Nick's morning visit and the Ministry inspection. The farmer tried his best not to show disappointment, but she knew his losses on the swine must be substantial.

'Surely you'll get compensation?' she

asked as they reached the house.

'Nothing to what I'd planned with them pigs,' was the dismal reply.

Mrs Medlicott welcomed Briony, her rosy cheeks belying the troubles she'd no doubt encountered over the past weeks. 'It's feeding time. See what you make of him, Miss Beaumont.' A cardboard box beside the roaring kitchen fire revealed Sarah's piglet. He lay still, his small, creased snout nuzzled in the warmth of a woolly blanket.

'He's not grown very much.' Briony bent down, instantly concerned by his lethargy. 'He's not drinking?'

'Won't suck half the time. I have to fairly force the teat down his throat.' Mrs Medlicott produced a baby's bottle filled with milk and a well-used rubber teat. As she picked the piglet up he gave a token struggle. She sat in an old armchair, bundled the piglet into the crook of her left arm and thrust the teat into his mouth.

Eagerly he began to suck, but after a

few minutes gave up the effort. 'There, you see what happens? He just loses all interest.' Mrs Medlicott coaxed, stroked and scratched the penny-sized ears. It was clear that she was very fond of her charge, and the beady black eyes fixed themselves upon her face as though she were his real mother.

'He's not up to much. I don't know why she bothers.' The farmer gave a hefty sigh and dismissed himself from the kitchen.

'Horace has got enough on his plate without worrying about Porky,' Mrs Medlicott excused. 'He's such a little love . . . I haven't the heart to give up on him.'

Briony took him into her arms, drawing her fingers over the furrowed pink head, so bald it was virtually shining. He smelt of milk and was as cuddly as a newborn baby. No wonder he was a favourite. Almost as if he knew how lovable he was, he sank with a wriggle or two into her chest, his nose rooting at her coat lapels.

When at last she returned him to Mrs Medlicott and another feed failed abysmally, her heart sank. She knew there wasn't very much she could do. Certainly there were no more drugs she could administer. Porky had a fifty-fifty chance, she imagined. A runt, if it pulled through, could often become a healthy specimen — but even then, where would the piglet end up? As long as people fried bacon with their eggs the likes of this baby pig were destined for an abrupt end. No doubt Mrs Medlicott understood and accepted the paradoxes of pig farming. She had lived with them for the last thirty years and managed a living. And, to prove their love for animals, Sarah and Seth had been spared. But as for Porky, darling though he was, perhaps fate would take his frail life into her own hands.

'I think you've done a wonderful job bringing him on this far, Mrs Medlicott. I couldn't imagine doing all those night feeds. I do hope he pulls through, for your sake.'

The farmer's wife looked up at her. Wise eyes told Briony she did not expect miracles. Her philosophy incorporated a kind heart, yet a practical mind. The piglet wriggled in her arms, his instincts telling him the warmth of the blazing fire and his makeshift box-sty was the better place to be.

Driving away from the Medlicotts' farm, Briony had the feeling she would be called back soon. There would be little she could do of course . . .

Going back to the surgery was an off-the-cuff decision. She was due to start her on-call duties early the following morning, so she decided to check in with Anita just in case anything had arisen. Besides, it was turning out too beautiful an evening to miss. The light was fading against a scarlet and purple horizon. As she wound the window down she smelt bonfires simmering in evening gardens, ripely fallen leaves roasting in the flames and winding into the air.

Besides, returning home would only result in her lazing in a bath to avoid getting in the way.

She drove into the car park, pulled on the brake and killed the engine. It was only as she was halfway in that she noticed Nick's car parked at the side-entrance. She imagined that after completing the calls he had shared with her he would return home and catch up on his sleep. Not more emergencies, surely?

She found Nick in his room. He stood still, his broad outline silhouetted against the window. For once he wasn't moving about the room but had stopped to savour the spectacular sunset.

'I didn't think I'd find you here,' Briony began, her heart racing as she saw him.

He swivelled on his heel, his eyes heavy-lided. 'You can come in, you know,' he told her, a soft ring to his voice. 'My mood has improved with the day.'

She smiled, moving in a few steps. 'You didn't manage to get any sleep?'

He shook his head. 'We had another two suspected SVD cases. As luck would have it, though, they both came to nothing. Let's hope the benighted episode is all over.'

'Yes . . . ' She thought in particular of the Medlicotts and how the outbreak had affected them. 'Do you think the SVD has anything to do with weakening the strain? Obviously the virus was about while Sarah was pregnant with her litter.'

'You mean would that little runt be healthy if it weren't for the SVD?'

She nodded, annoyed with herself for becoming so involved in the Medlicotts' fortunes. She shouldn't, of course. Farmers risked their livelihoods every day of the week, and the loss — or survival — of one tiny piglet wasn't going to ruin anyone.

Nick chuckled under his breath. 'You're quite a softy at heart, aren't you? I wouldn't mind betting you've called in there today to see how he's doing.'

Pink stole, unbidden, into her face. 'As a matter of fact, I did.' To offset the disagreeable sensation that he was looking right through her, she walked to the window and, standing by him, valiantly tried to change the topic. 'I was just about to have a look through tomorrow's appointments . . .'

He wasn't to be put off. 'To answer your question about Sarah's litter, because I know you're worrying — I don't think the virus in particular is responsible for the weakling. And there isn't, of course, anything more you can do, just in case you're holding yourself responsible.'

'No . . . I'm not, but I don't like the feeling of inadequacy. Piglets die all the time. They get crushed, or suffocated, and there's nothing you can do except suggest more precautionary farrowing procedures. But when a tiny little runt tries so hard to cling on to life, and there's nothing you can do to help, it's almost too painful to accept.'

He moved closer and wound an arm around her shoulders, making her heart lurch in a wave of need. It was only a friendly gesture because he was being sympathetic, but he didn't realise what he was doing to her. He said gently, 'It is natural, you know, to become fond of your patients. It's not a crime. We all do it occasionally. I know that little piglet has stirred more in you than you like to admit. And don't deny it, I can see it in your eyes.'

'What,' she spluttered, laughing and rushing into nervous conversation, 'can you possibly see in my eyes?'

The large hands were suddenly turning her around to face him. She looked up, at the knotted forehead embellished by a great shock of black hair.

'I can see a lot in those eyes of yours which leads me to believe you're not quite who you say you are.'

'That's because it's the end of the day and I'm beginning to feel tired and hungry,' she joked. But her laughter rang as empty as her words. For her response to his unexpected gentleness was devastating. She waited for a moment, hardly daring to swallow, watching the passage of his eyes across her face as if to detect her inner feelings.

'It's all going on up here, isn't it?' he smiled perceptively, his fingers solidly warm on her arms causing the persistent thudding in her stomach to increase. 'In that brain of yours,' he murmured, 'tick, tock, this way, that way . . .'

Somehow she knew he wouldn't kiss her. At least, not on the lips. For which she was thankful, for just at that moment she couldn't have endured another immense crescendo of heartbeat. His lips fell, soft as spring, on her forehead, and she gazed up at him. Was this sympathy, or kindness . . . or, what was even worse, had he kissed her like that because there was nothing else he could think of to do in the face of her absurd sentimentality over an animal?

Hot on the heels of disappointment rushed another mental question posed by an inner voice which had been nagging all day. What did she want at this point in her life? What was her direction, her goals and her aims? Ambition, the need to assert her independence, seemed temporarily to have been forgotten.

What you really want, Briony Beaumont, she told herself, grateful that her admission was a silent one, is to be scooped into those arms, carried out into the hall right under Lea's nose and be swept off, where they could be alone, where schedules and timetables and the urgency and seriousness of work was left behind . . . just for a few hours. That their lives, just for once, would stop teeming with people and animals.

But naturally it wouldn't happen.

Having dispensed quickly with the vision, she just as quickly began hoping for second best — that the deliciously warm lips would return in the direction of her mouth.

But it was then, precisely then, that the shadow fell upon them. Not exactly a shadow, Briony realised, more an undeniable aura from the doorway. It stood six feet tall, and when she looked she saw that it was possessed of an expensive grey suit and an austere regimental tie embossed with a coat of arms. Crowning the erect body was a familiar, distinguished head of silver-grey hair.

'Father!' Briony gasped, still in Nick's arms. 'And Matthew!'

A sudden flash in the eyes of the younger man warned her that he was there like some sort of rear-guard preparing for action. The petulant expression on his face struck her as extremely stuffy, and had not her father looked so daunting she would have been hard put to it not to laugh outright.

'H-how lovely to see you both!' And, managing to free herself from Nick, she added gingerly, 'Do come in . . . please.'

Her offer was not taken up, so she walked to her father, standing on tiptoe to kiss the unbending cheek. Ralph Beaumont stiffened as his daughter embraced him, his eyes slipping down to regard her with incredulity.

'Have you lost your senses, Briony?' His voice held a biting, controlled anger. 'I came here not knowing what to expect . . . but I never believed I'd find you in the arms of a Lloyd!'

She stared at him, her eyes widening as her breath locked in her throat. 'You don't understand — '

'I understand very well what I see with my own eyes.'

She shook her head, giving a croaky little laugh, her protestation dying on the tip of her tongue.

'Do you realise I've not heard one word from you since your birthday? Nine months ago, to be precise. Is this what our relationship is dwindling to? Christmas and birthdays?'

'That's silly . . . I was coming to see

you — just as soon as I'd settled . . . '

'Don't argue with me, Briony. Get your things together. I want to talk to you — and I don't intend doing it here, in this place.'

She couldn't believe he was taking such an attitude. She had expected him to be disturbed about her working for Nick, a lecture perhaps or a tirade even, blowing itself out eventually, but not this deliberate insistence on treating her like a twelve-year-old.

'Since you refuse to pay me the courtesy of coming to Amberfields I'm forced to take valuable time away from my business interests to come here today.'

It was at this point that Matthew, rather unwisely, stepped forward. Before he had time to move again Nick was there beside her, his arm slipping around her waist. His profile was hard and unbending, his stare focused on Matthew. Briony realised she was completely surrounded by men. Incredulity tugged at the corners of her mouth as she thought of the absurdity of the situation.

'Mr Beaumont,' Nick intervened, switching his attention to her father, 'Briony is a very busy young woman herself. I would imagine she's no less committed to her work than you are to yours.'

Ralph Beaumont tensed, his blue eyes glinting. 'Keep out of this,' he warned in a cold voice. 'Briony's affairs are none of your business.'

'I'm afraid I have to disagree with you,' Nick drawled calmly. 'I assure you they are. And I suggest you listen to what Briony has to say for once.'

The older man's face grew very red under the distinguished whiteness of his hair. Briony thought she saw his fists clench for a moment, and as her gaze travelled up to Matthew, with a start she realised that his features displayed openly the ill-concealed spitefulness which she had suspected in his nature. He said in a tight voice, 'Briony, please do as your father tells you. It's useless trying to have a discussion here. The least you can do is talk to us . . . in private.'

Briony opened her mouth, but Nick stiffened, his fingers tightening on her waist. Her automatic reaction was that she couldn't really believe this was going on.

'Briony . . . ' began Matthew, his voice trailing.

'Keep out of this, Prior,' Nick warned.

Ralph Beaumont straightened his shoulders, muttering under his breath, and Briony saw, with a recoil of her stomach, the intensity of his anger flicker in his eyes.

'Briony isn't a child any longer, Mr Beaumont.' She watched Nick's mouth move, barely hearing what he said, she was so worried the situation might take a turn for the worse. The air was electric. 'She has a mind of her own. The mind of a fully grown and highly intelligent young woman.'

Shock creased her father's face. He turned to her. 'Briony, for the last time, come to your senses! Don't be foolishly duped by a troublemaker you should have had the sense to ignore like the plague!'

'Listen to your father, Briony,' Matthew bleated. 'He's only thinking of what's best for you.'

The best, she thought with an icy shiver, always had to do with money in her father's mind. Matthew could not have said a truer word. Her father was a wealthy man and, no doubt like all rich men, he thought his wealth entitled him to whatever he wanted in life. He had never given up trying to buy back his children. Perhaps that was why her desire to show him she was independent had resulted in an obsessive predilection about her career.

Nick moved an inch in front of her. She glanced at his face, devoid of expression. 'Mr Beaumont, I think there's something you should know. It really makes this conversation quite irrelevant.'

She could hardly believe what she

was hearing as, to her utter amazement, he added with chill civility, 'Briony and I are engaged to be married. We haven't decided on the date yet . . . but when we do, I assure you, you'll be the first to know.'

8

'I can't believe what I've just heard!'
Briony spluttered, hurrying to the
window to watch her father and
Matthew climb into the sleek, dark blue
Bentley.

Calmly, Nick dug his hands into his
pockets, watching her. 'You're over-
reacting. Sit down and get your second
wind.'

She turned to stare at him. 'I'm
over-reacting? Nick, you just told my
father an outright lie . . . that we're
engaged to be married! What's my
reaction supposed to be, then?' Heaven
alone knew why she hadn't spoken up.
But what could she have said? Her
father hadn't been listening anyway.
'Why did you tell him we were
engaged?'

'I would have thought it perfectly
obvious.'

'Not to me it isn't.'

'Then if you sit down . . . take a deep breath and stop panicking, I'll explain.'

She was torn by the urge to run after the car now streaking out of the car park and the more appealing suggestion of Nick's. Appealing, because it would mean she didn't make a complete fool of herself, running outside and waving her arms like a lunatic.

She sat, begrudgingly, on a chair.

Nick grinned, and sat down too. 'It's all very straightforward when you think it out logically . . . '

'Logically!' Briony's blue eyes flashed.

'Yes, exactly that. Now forgive me, but it does seem too obvious for words that your father had no intention of allowing you to make up your own mind.'

'No . . . but perhaps — '

'There's no 'perhaps' about it, Briony,' Nick interrupted and something in his voice made her stiffen and look at him. 'He would have persuaded you out of knowing your own mind. You

210

treated his approach too lightly.'

She shook her head. 'I could have talked him out of his mood. He would have listened.'

Nick frowned at her. 'Do you really believe that?'

'Well . . . it might have taken a while . . . '

'It wouldn't have worked. He isn't used to no being said to him. Now you're back in Bagbourne he expects you to behave as if nothing has changed.'

'But a lot has changed!'

Nick's dark eyes glittered as he agreed, 'I know that. You know that. But does your father understand? I'm sure he still believes you're the child who left home — and has now returned to pick up the pieces where she left off. Just look at the way he was talking to you. Time has stood still for him.'

She had no reply to that, for deep in her heart she knew it was true. Wasn't that why she had limited her visits to home? Long-distance phone calls had been so much easier — and safer. It was impossible to stop the flood of certainty that rushed through her at the truth of Nick's words.

'You didn't have to say we were engaged,' she mumbled, 'you didn't have to go that far.' A wild sweep of colour cascaded through her cheeks as she said the word. She lifted her hand to push back the tumbling waves of hair falling untidily across her burning cheeks. The one curse of having reddish hair was that every inner emotion was so painfully obvious.

'Have you a more watertight suggestion?' Nick sat back in his chair, looking at her, his long brown fingers entwined thoughtfully under his chin.

'You make what you said sound almost sensible.'

'It is — sensible for you.'

'And now you're going to tell me you said it purely for my sake.'

He smiled, the white, even teeth appearing briefly as his lips lifted. 'OK, for mine too. If you're left in peace, you'll be able to concentrate on your job. And Prior will leave you alone too.'

Briony's eyebrows lifted sharply. 'What makes you think I want him to leave me alone?'

'Because now it's obvious he's your father's man. Surely you can see it?'

'So to spite him . . . and Father . . . you've used me?' Could it be true? Was Nick using the situation to get back at her family?'

'I doubt if I deserve the credit for masterminding such a plan,' Nick grinned, getting up out of his chair.

Whether it was weakness or cowardice she didn't know, but she decided not to press the point. She got up, feeling drained. If she hadn't decided to come back to the practice tonight, none of this would have happened. Or, she thought, with sudden horror, would Matthew and her father have come out to Don's? The picture of them all thrashing it out in front of Beth made her heart heave. For a split-second she was grateful that the confrontation had happened here, and just a little grateful, too, that Nick had resolved the problem.

It was hard to imagine that this whole episode in her life had begun by her throwing herself at him — literally!

'This . . . this engagement,' she stammered, aware of the weakness in her stomach; 'how do you propose to go about it?'

He laughed, casually throwing back his head. 'Simple. We pretend. It won't be so difficult. If anyone asks we repeat what we told your father.'

Her eyes widened, and before she could say anything he raised his hands, palms towards her. 'It's foolproof, if we both stick to the same story.' He gave a grin. 'And when our working arrangement comes to an end and you move off to pastures green you can have the pleasure of jilting me.'

For a moment a bleak emptiness belied the amusement in his eyes, but he recovered quickly, adding, 'A sort of compensation prize for all the discomfort you've had to suffer.'

She raised her chin. 'I believe engagements are a promise. And I don't believe in breaking promises.'

Quietly he regarded her. 'Really? Most people these days have a more . . . liberal attitude towards sex and marriage.'

She decided the conversation was taking a decided turn for the worse. 'I wasn't talking about sex. I was talking about the promise of a lifelong commitment,' she answered shortly, getting up.

She had reached the door when Nick called, 'You're an old-fashioned girl at heart, are you? I must have read you wrong.'

'I suppose you must have. I'm old-fashioned enough to believe marriage should be taken seriously . . . and I feel immensely guilty that we're doing just the opposite.'

'But we're only making believe! To get out of a difficult situation.'

She turned to stare at him. Why, for goodness' sake, didn't she just tell him it was a rotten idea and that she was going to see her father and put matters right?

Cowardice prevailing, she thought better of it; better the devil you knew than the one you didn't? 'Well, I suppose there's not much I can do now anyway. I just hope the idea doesn't rebound somehow.'

Nick walked to the door, his arm brushing hers, and predictably the movement caused her nerves to jingle. He said with wry amusement in his eyes, 'Trust me,' then slid a smile towards her, a hint of sensuality coming in the full lower lip against the curved upper one.

'Goodnight,' she said quickly.

'I shan't see you tomorrow.' He was still watching her as she started up the hall. 'I've a day on calls. And I think you're fully booked with appointments here.'

Walking to the car, Briony realised she hadn't thought to check the appointments book. Nick must have. There was very little, it seemed, if anything, that missed him.

As she turned the engine into life, the relevance of the thought became clearer. He was a forward thinker, a planner. The matter of the engagement had come so spontaneously that even her father had looked devastated by it.

But had Nick just drawn the idea out of the blue? Now, engaging second gear with a hefty clunk as the car ascended the hill to home, she wondered. He was a clever, powerful, resourceful man. Look at how he had interfered in her life from the word go — and how she had let him!

The thought niggled like a pebble in her shoe. For a while she forgot about it. But then, its edges digging into her consciousness, it brought her up sharply. Unlike the stone, it could not be thrown away.

*   *   *

On a cold grey morning well into the middle of November, a few lily-white flakes of snow dusted the window-panes of the surgery. Henry Dappledale, grinning under a cloth cap and dropping chunks of slushy mud from his boots, strode out of Nick's room. A smile stretched from ear to ear. 'I'll count on you, then, Nick.'

Then the slam of a door.

Heavily involved in a busy morning of small operations, Briony left the theatre — and almost bumped into him. He came towards her, raising a weather-beaten hand, clapping her on the back. 'Congratulations from the missus and me,' he boomed, in a voice that rang through every room. 'Mind, I said to the missus I thought it'd be the young 'un, not the boss himself.' The farmer winked. 'He's a good 'un, your Nick, no mistake.'

Briony stared at him, her heart beginning to thud in the back of her throat. 'My . . . what?'

'You and him! Who else would I be talking about?'

Enlightenment dawned. A flood of

mortified colour stole up from her neck.

'How . . . how did you know?' she asked in a whisper, hoping none of the staff could hear. But simultaneously people seemed to appear from the woodwork.

' 'Bout your engagement.' Henry's voice soared an octave. 'Whole town knows! Was it supposed to be a secret, then?'

Briony tried to shake her head, but movement eluded her. She should have known better than to think the engagement could be kept quiet.

The farmer tilted back his cap. 'Well, no use standing here twiddling my thumbs. Better get around to what I've come for. Old Medlicott is thinking of packing his pigs in; did you know that?'

'No — no, I didn't.'

She wasn't sure whom she felt most annoyed with, Nick and his brainwave, Mr Dappledale for broadcasting it, or herself for being so gullible. She shook her head, trying to take up the threads of the conversation.

'Could've happened to any of us.' He shuffled uncomfortably in front of her. 'So I reckon it's time the town pulled its weight. Me and your fiancé — ' he said the word with relish ' — we thought about raising money for some new pigs. A Christmas knees-up. Get everybody to come . . . it'll do us good to have a shindig, and it'll be for a deserving cause.'

'Sounds lovely,' Briony mumbled without enthusiasm, praying he wouldn't return to the subject she dreaded. 'I'd like to stop and discuss it with you, but I'm a bit behind time, I'm afraid.' She edged past him.

'Yes, time is money!' The farmer tipped his cap. 'By the way, those scouring calves you did, they're top of the tree now. I won't be opposed to having a female vet again.'

He left with a wake of mud zigzagging the floor.

A deadly silence reigned.

Briony bolted for her room, brazening out the rest of the morning avoiding the curious glances. But Anita's grin spoke volumes, which meant probably the whole staff had heard!

'You're a dark horse,' the young nurse laughed. 'Congratulations . . . though obviously it's a bit late.'

'No . . . not late at all! I — er — that is, we — haven't actually planned anything at all . . . yet,' Briony muttered, and was thankful that Lea did not seem to be around. What in heaven's name would she think? And what precisely would she do about the situation? She could hardly know that it was all a lie . . . or had Nick told her, somehow persuaded her to fall in with his scheme? The possibilities were so numerous that her brain began to ache.

At lunchtime she fled to the nearby park, sitting on a freezing-cold bench, preferring hypothermia to the curious interrogation of staff. Tiny snowflakes, thicker now, like cotton-wool puffs, spread as a blanket, untrodden across the grass. The fir trees spread their branches, frost-white fingers dripping their moisture, and a lumpy grey sky reflected her mood. Soon everyone would know. Beth and Don too — if they didn't already? She had made Nick promise they would keep the engagement quiet if possible. He'd actually told her there was nothing to worry about. The rat! Had he deliberately spread it about?

Collar up to her chin, her coppery hair tied high up on her head, her cheeks fanned by emotion, Briony sat on the bench gritting her teeth against the cold . . . thinking.

* * *

'A barn dance? In December? You've got to be joking!' Ben sat back in his chair, fair hair flopping.

Perched on the edge of his desk, Nick studied the faces of his staff. The meeting was almost over, and a ripple

222

of amusement circulated the room.

'No, Ben, I'm deadly serious. It's the only idea Henry Dappledale and I could come up with to help Medlicott out of a sticky patch. A barn dance will be different, I grant you, but perhaps that will attract people at this time of year.'

Lea, her violet eyes sparkling as she sat directly by Nick, said, 'We'll freeze, surely?'

Briony sat on her fingers to revive them from the cold. She had taken a chair at the back of the room, but Lea seemed somehow to turn around and slide her a glance every so often.

'Horace Medlicott's willing to provide a building wired for electricity,' Nick was explaining. 'It used to be his barn, but when his new one was built he converted this into a shed for his equipment. He uses the place for all his repairs.'

'Not exactly the Ritz, but I suppose it'll have to do,' Lea grumbled disappointedly. Crossing her legs with the grace of a gazelle, she smiled up at Nick.

Briony froze. She was flirting with him! Even though it was general knowledge now that he and Briony were engaged, she had the nerve to sit there and flirt!

Desperately afraid of revealing her annoyance, Briony imagined a cool — a cold shower, as soon as she got home from work. What in heaven's name was the matter with her? She should be delighted with the way Lea still responded to Nick, drooling over his every word. It meant that she must know the engagement was a sham, that he had taken her into his confidence. But what else had she expected? Was she gullible enough, even for one second, to imagine that there had been a grain of truth in Nick's outlandish statement to her father? Hadn't his words been something in the order of allowing her to jilt him when she left the practice?

But did he have to pander to Lea like that? By the way he was talking to her, that smile changing the whole character of his face, he intended to go on in front of the other members of staff, just the way he always had, despite the fact that the engagement was common knowledge.

She jumped as she realised everyone was looking at her. 'I . . . I'm sorry, what . . . ?'

'I asked you, Briony,' Nick said slowly as though he were speaking so that she could lip-read, 'if you and Beth could organise the food?'

She crimsoned, but she managed to gather herself, to form an expression on her face which reflected nothing of the anger concealed behind her blue eyes. 'Yes, yes, of course.'

'Most people will bring home-made food and we can set up trestle-tables. It'll be a question of making out lists, nothing too difficult.'

Remembering that this was supposed to be her fiancé, even if he had forgotten, she switched on a smile. 'I'll do my best.'

'I'm sure you will,' Nick smiled blandly back.

Whoever's going to be fooled by this kind of repartee? she wondered, turning away from Lea's gaze.

The whole room seemed to be watching them. Again that sideways glance from Lea, violet eyes dancing triumphantly, making Briony's skin crawl.

Luckily Ben broke the silence. 'I'll help Dappledale with plonk, if you like, Nick?' He gestured to the girls with a grin. 'A punch, for instance. We'll rustle up something with a sting in its tail, shall we?'

The room burst into laughter as insults were rife. Nick said at last, winding up the meeting, 'How about the second week in December? Does that give us enough time?'

The vote was unanimous. Nick nodded, his glance slipping down to Lea as she drew him into conversation.

The place emptied, and Briony found herself still sitting on her seat watching them, her eyes furtively taking in Lea's body language, and, feeling quite sick, she realised she simply couldn't drag her eyes away. She was transfixed. Trying to motivate herself, she found she was glaring at Nick. Lea got up, moving slowly, her hand touching Nick's arm.

When she had gone, Briony held Nick's gaze. He was outrageous! As though butter wouldn't melt in his mouth! Flirting like that. And now he was calmly smiling with cool mockery in his eyes.

'What's wrong?' he asked, frowning at her.

'There's nothing wrong as far as I'm concerned.' He knew exactly what was wrong — it would be all the same if they really were engaged!

He walked over and leaned casually, his broad back resting against the wall, arms folded across his chest. Her heart made the most enormous leap. He said, laughing, 'You'll never make an actress, Briony. You were looking daggers at me and we're supposed to be engaged!'

'It was your idea, not mine.'

'You didn't disagree with it.'

'I couldn't. But I don't have to like it.'

He shrugged. 'Just don't take it out on Lea. She's doing her damnedest to be civil, and you're ostracising her.'

Briony gasped as anger flushed her cheeks. 'I'm ostracising her? That's a joke! She's the one who's ignoring me and making up to you deliberately!'

The dark eyes suddenly lit up as he chuckled throatily.

'What's so funny?'

'Do you know this is the first time you've allowed yourself to show signs of being purely human? You're not a paragon of virtue after all. You're jealous as hell!'

Warning bells began to clang noisily inside her. She was making a fool of herself . . . she had to stop this insanity and act like a rational human being.

Behaving like a deceived wife was ludicrous!

He said, not bothering to mince words, 'Why don't you let yourself go a little? Have some fun.'

'Fun, you call this?' In spite of her capable reasoning she was losing control. 'I don't want to be one of a procession of women in your life, even under the guise of a theatrical performance.'

'Ah, now we're getting to the truth.' His mockery hurt her so much that she began to walk away, but he caught hold of her wrist. 'Come on, let's have the truth.'

'I . . . I don't know what you're talking about.'

'This procession of women? Do you mind naming a few names . . . just so I know who I'm supposed to have seduced?'

Her temper snapped at his flaunted innocence. 'I know about Samantha Forbes. And I know that you'll drop Lea as soon as it suits you — you're that kind of person. You can't help it, I suppose. You're obsessed with arranging people's lives to suit your own purposes, and ... ' the words came tumbling out so fast she could hardly breathe ' ... and I don't want to be part of it. I don't intend to fall into the category of ... '

'Of what?'

'N-nothing,' she stammered. 'It isn't important.'

Hardly breathing, she felt his fingers tighten around her wrist, and then, as he decided to let her go, he began to laugh. His laughter drifted easily until he saw her lips twitch in humiliation. 'Ah, we've touched a sensitive spot, have we? You put yourself a cut above the average female?'

'That's not what I meant at all!'

To her chagrin Nick walked casually to the door, amusement wrinkling his brow as he turned back. 'You're a funny girl, Briony ... no woman has ever made me laugh the way you do.'

When he was gone she let out a sigh,

breathing so hard that she felt as though she had run a marathon. Covering her eyes with her hands, she tried to think what she had said. What was it that was so funny? She'd expected anger from him, affronted denials about his behaviour. But he'd merely laughed at her! She would become neurotic if she went on like this!

As her hands dropped down, mentally she amended that thought. It was not Nick prompting her to react so neurotically, it was jealousy. Overpowering jealousy of Lea!

She sank back against the wall. His touch had numbed her; the place where his fingers had been on her wrist tingled. She was aching — aching with such intensity that her insides were raw, as though someone were twisting her stomach. Deliberately, all her life she had held herself back from emotional commitment. Now she was no longer her own person, she was someone she hardly recognised!

* * *

Don had let Phoebe out to exercise for a brief while.

Briony gazed from her bedroom window, staring absent-mindedly at the view. The weather forecast was right — the skies looked heavy and changeable. An odd morning. More snow, probably, and the sludge of the previous fall had barely cleared.

Phoebe whinnied and raised her sleek head almost as if she knew she was being watched. How on earth was Don going to reconcile selling her? She meant more to him than any of the other horses. Briony shivered and tried to put aside useless thoughts. For a few seconds she watched a pale light flicker in the sky, a ghost of a sun, quickly extinguished by thick grey clouds.

Don appeared, calling to Phoebe. She trotted eagerly towards him, her nostrils flaring in recognition, and Briony turned away, reminding herself that she had enough worries of her own without thinking of her brother's.

The weekend over, she closed the window, trying to close a window of her heart. Two days spent under the scrutiny of Beth had done nothing to help. The engagement had been a non-stop subject, and she was thankful now Monday morning had come.

At work, she began her list with two straightforward spayings. Then came an aged dachshund with lymphosarcoma which she had been treating with corticosteroids. Finally a young man brought in a rather unusual case, a St Bernard puppy with a nasty deviation of both forefeet.

'I think I'd like a second opinion on this St Bernard,' she told Anita as the man waited in her consulting-room. 'I don't know if Lea has dealt with a carpal valgus before?'

'I'm not sure, actually. As it's her day off I can't ask . . . but Nick has just arrived. When he's finished on the phone, shall I ask him to come in?'

'All right. If he's not too busy.'

Nick appeared shortly, and to Briony's relief gave her a smile. Somehow she'd built it up in her mind that after the staff meeting Monday was going to be an uphill struggle, but her nervousness dispelled. Calmly as always, he examined the puppy, and after a few moments took her to one side.

'He's under six months, isn't he? I think we could surgically tackle the problem.'

She hesitated. 'It's not worth waiting until he's older?'

'We'd have to wait until he's skeletally mature. And then it would mean moving a suitable wedge of bone from the radius. The surgery's even more complex. As he's only just over four months I'd prefer to make the correction now, while he's growing. If you haven't done an osteochondrosis before, it'll be good experience. Make the appointment for a week's time . . . and perhaps you'd like to act as anaesthetist for me?'

It was a thoughtful gesture. He made

it so as not to demean her profession-
ally, yet not leaving her out on a limb as
far as performing the intricate surgery
was concerned.

'Yes, I'd like that very much,' she
answered with a grateful smile.

After the appointment had been
made she was about to eat sandwiches
in the staffroom, thankful that Lea had
taken the Monday off. The girls had
been discussing Christmas shopping
— it would be good to relax without
wondering if she was going to be
cornered in front of the staff. But as she
was about to ascend the stairs Nick
touched her arm. 'Eating alone?'

'No, with the girls. Why, is something
wrong?'

'Look . . . I might as well come
straight to the point.'

Briony's heart lept. She knew instantly
that it was bad news, though of what
category she wasn't sure.

'That was Medlicott on the phone.
Your little protégé, I'm afraid, is going
downhill fast.'

Briony nodded quietly. She had known it would come. It was silly to be upset. 'I'm not surprised.'

'Do you want to go out there?'

She nodded, retracing her steps. 'Yes. If he's struggling I'll have to put him down. I don't think Mrs Medlicott would want to see him suffer.'

'I'll come with you.'

'No,' she objected sharply, 'you don't have to do that.'

'I know I don't, but I'll come all the same. I wanted to check on his pigs anyway.' Briony looked into the concerned face and felt her heart melt, just as the snow had done in the paddock this morning as she had taken that first early glance. He had the same effect on her. And there wasn't a thing she could do about it!

'We'll go in my car. Have you much on this afternoon?' Nick was already gathering his things together, walking towards the dispensary for drugs.

'No, I'll arrange things with the girls. Ben's in for an hour or two, I believe.

It was only minutes before she had bundled her case into the BMW and Nick was driving from the practice, his face set in hard lines. To her immense relief he did all the talking. Drawing a long breath, she tried to relax, gathering her thoughts as he spoke. Preparing herself for the task ahead, she was glad of the distraction.

At the farm Horace Medlicott edged his tractor to a standstill and jumped down to greet them, wiping a mucky cloth across his forehead. Even under threat of grey skies and snow, he wore only a body-warmer and a thick shirt. He nodded to the farmhouse. 'The wife will make you a cuppa when you're finished.'

Mrs Medlicott bustled as usual in her warm kitchen, only the slightest change in her face, a pallor which was not her usual colour. She smiled apologetically. 'Sorry to bring you out again.'

Porky lay in his box. Briony knew at once that his struggle was almost over and to prolong it would only be unkind.

She knelt beside the box, and felt Nick's fingers tighten on her shoulder. Then he was gone, and Mrs Medlicott was putting on the kettle, clattering dishes into the sink.

Briony opened her case. The farmer's wife stopped, briefly, glanced across the room to the roaring fire. 'He was a real old soldier, that one.'

For a moment Briony's reaction was one of sadness, a tug at her heart that always brought a lump to her throat. But then her professionalism took over, and carefully she drifted the tiny pig into sleep. No doubt there would be many more occasions in her life like this. She thought of Greg Harding and how he had helped her come to terms with this part of the work. His old-fashioned philosophies had been a sort of standing joke among the locals. Greg toasted off all his departed animals with a jug of best bitter, unafraid to make it clear that he thought every living spirit was accompanied by a soul. Not that Briony ever

238

took him seriously, for he was a Dalesman who possessed a rare sense of humour. However, she too liked to think of life — and death — in this way. Visualising Greg now, she realised how much like Nick he was in his ways, though she had never consciously been aware of it. Not until now, when Nick had thoughtfully intimated his support by touching her shoulder.

Half an hour later, Briony was sitting across the table from Nick and Mrs Medlicott had her radio tuned in to a lively requests programme. Horace Medlicott washed his forearms at the sink, chatting to his wife about the ditch he had been dragging during the morning. Life was back to normal again, for farming went on continuously, despite earthquakes.

Mrs Medlicott set hot tea and crumpets, thickly buttered, on to the table. 'How's the rest of those terrors doing?' she asked Nick, dragging out a chair to sit beside him.

'Spectacularly well, I have to say. All

Sophie's piglets are weaned, and I'm coming out soon to castrate the males.'

'We don't want boar taint after the SVD,' agreed Mr Medlicott, plunging into the crumpets. Briony knew the rather unpleasant procedure had to be performed or the pork would eventually be tainted. Horace Medlicott never attempted this himself, as many back-yard pig-keepers did to try to save expense. He treated his pigs, as Nick had once observed, like humans. Perhaps that was why he had such a startling rate of success.

Just as Briony was to sink her teeth into the butter-coated snack, Mrs Medlicott rubbed her hands down her pinny and very auspiciously remarked, 'I hear it's congratulations to you both. Why, you kept that a good secret, didn't you?'

The blood rushed to Briony's neck and then into her face. She saw Nick grinning, enjoying her embarrassment.

'Oh, no secret, Mrs Medlicott,' he told her, as though it was an everyday occurrence. 'We just didn't get around to announcing it before. What with one thing and another we've been pretty busy.'

'No wonder you couldn't wait to get home,' Mrs Medlicott giggled, looking at Briony. 'You all the way up there in the north, and him down here.'

'Oh, no,' Briony began, 'it wasn't quite like that . . .'

'Henry Dappledale told us all about it,' the lady chattered on, drawing a knife over more crumpets for a second layer of butter. 'Childhood sweethearts, wasn't it? That's romance for you. I always said it, didn't I, Horace? I always said they made a good couple from the moment I saw them, the day Sarah tipped Mr Lloyd off his feet into the manure pile.'

A brief silence encompassed the table as even Horace Medlicott reddened at his wife's words. But then, to Briony's immense relief, they were all laughing, and Nick's eyes sparkled as he gazed at her.

'A white wedding, I hope,' grinned Mrs Medlicott.

'With all the county to see you both off,' added her husband.

Nick nodded. 'Whatever Briony decides. But I'm hoping we'll have St Martin's. The organ is second only to the cathedral, you know. And though it's a small church, it's one we were both baptised in.'

Briony's jaw dropped. 'H-how do you know I was baptised at St Martin's?'

'Darling . . . ' Nick sighed with mock impatience, ' . . . your memory is shocking. Weren't we discussing it only last week?'

'But — '

'Nerves does that,' Mrs Medlicott interrupted, her rosy cheeks beaming. 'Pre-wedding nerves. Don't you worry, my girl, it'll all turn out right on the day, you mark my words.'

Briony nodded dumbly, furious with Nick.

Hardly able to wait until they left the Medlicotts', she finished her tea with a

242

gulp. Once outside, he gripped her arm and propelled her to the BMW. 'Don't make a scene — they're watching from the window.'

With extreme difficulty she waited until they were in the car. But before she could tell him exactly what she thought he started up the engine. 'Don told me about St Martin's — we just happened to be discussing the subject of births, marriages and deaths. And, as for spinning the little story to Mrs Medlicott, I thought it would do her the world of good. She needed cheering up.'

'I . . . I can't believe you're serious!' Briony gasped, finding it hard not to burst into laughter.

'I'm not — that's the point. Remember, we're indulging in fantasy. Besides, you can't honestly tell me you wouldn't like to be married in an historic little church like St Martin's with the organ rattling out the Wedding March at full blast!'

'Well, of course I would . . . I

mean . . . no! Of course I wouldn't . . . '

'Quiet now, there's a good girl — looks as if we're up to our chins in diversions. The road's blocked off. It must have snowed pretty badly down this way during the afternoon.'

Briony sat quite still, listening to the thump of her heart. Whatever would the Medlicotts think later, when the truth was out? And not just the Medlicotts, but everyone! If this was the kind of thing Nick was going to do . . .

A while later, when diversions had been followed, snowdrifts avoided and a sanded road discovered, Nick turned his face briefly towards her. 'You're quiet.'

'I know I'm quiet. I'm recovering.'

'I'm sorry about the piglet. There was absolutely nothing else you could do.'

'No . . . it's not that I'm recovering from.'

'Well, if it's what I said to the Medlicotts, it was only fun. I really don't intend rumours to spread.'

She ignored this one. Bagbourne could never resist gossip — of any kind. The grapevine was its mainstay, as she supposed was the same in all small villages and towns. Nick must know that too. But what she was concerned about was the way she had felt when Nick wove his story. Sudden exhilaration had caught her up, excitement had rendered her breathless. Nick's fiancée . . . she, Briony Beaumont. Engaged to be married in St Martin's, in white, with the organ ringing out.

'Say something. I'd prefer you to be biting my head off rather than sitting there so quietly.'

She wound down the window to give herself some air. How could she possibly tell him what she was thinking? A fall of icy moisture spotted her face. 'It's snowing again,' she prevaricated, winding down the window fully. Overhead the sky was a thick grey blanket no doubt waiting to be shaken of its contents.

'I'd better call back at my place and collect a change of clothing. I didn't bargain for this. I've two more farm visits when I get back.'

And, staring blindly ahead of her, Briony watched the BMW's nose sneak off the main road towards Bagbourne and begin the descent into the valley of white.

In ten minutes they reached the house. She saw large bay windows, surrounded with red brick, and the neat, pale imprints under the snow of flower-bedded gardens. Then came low grey stone walls, a hearty oak front door under an eaved porch. Her first and most irreconcilable thought was, Is this where he brings Lea?

He said, as the engine died, 'Come in. You'll freeze out here.'

He opened her door, grabbed her arm, and soon, through the snow, they were walking to the house. It was, Briony thought, an afternoon of piercing beauty, the pointed pinnacles of fir trees drooping white, the snow bearing down in heavier drifts as they crunched along the path. When he opened the front door, the first object that met her eyes was a photograph encompassed in a silver frame, quite a large one, strategically positioned on a refectory table.

Nick shook snow from his shoes and smiled. Gazing at the photograph which he saw had taken her attention, he said, quite unrepentantly, 'That's Samantha. She's a stunning girl, isn't she?'

9

'Make yourself comfortable in the lounge,' said Nick. 'There's an instant log fire in there.'

Briony watched him take the stairs two at a time. When he disappeared, she moved closer to the photograph. So this was Samantha Forbes. The young woman smiled back at her. Deep-set, immensely confident eyes, rich chestnut hair. The man beside her, his arm linked around her waist ... was it Nick? For a minute she thought so, then when she looked closer she saw it was a stranger, darkly bearded. Shocked that she felt such deep relief that it wasn't Nick, she jumped as a noise came from upstairs.

Trying to shake off the shock, she tore herself away from the photograph and walked into the comfortable lounge. She saw books, bookcases full of them, chintz-covered armchairs, a battered but elegant leather chesterfield and at the far end of the room a roughly cut red brick hearth. Her eye went straight to the photographs above. She didn't want to look at them, but curiosity drove her forward.

She recognised Sebastian at once. He stood upright with his two young teenage sons beside him. Nick regarded the photographer solemnly. Luke, stockier and more self-assured, parted his lips in a broad smile. Then there were photos of dogs, Labradors and retrievers, and one of an older woman in a mahogany frame, so like Nick that it could be mistaken for no one else but his mother. Small and delicate with magnificent dark eyes, she stood alone in a country garden filled with flowers. Something about her reminded Briony of her own mother — perhaps the calm quietness of the eyes, the wistful smile. How on earth had they managed to cope with their handfuls of husbands?

'I told you, didn't I, that my mother died before I had a chance to settle back in Bagbourne?'

She started, turning around quickly, feeling a little as though she had been caught in the act of spying. Nick had changed his clothes. He now wore dark green cords and a thick woollen fishing jumper.

'You must have missed her a great deal.'

He nodded. 'I did, very much. Those were her dogs . . . she was crazy about animals.'

Briony glanced back, remembering her own childhood and the spaniels that had been her constant companions at Amberfields. 'It's surprising our mothers never met. I think they would have got on rather well.'

'They had a lot in common.' Nick raised a dark eyebrow. 'Extremely obstinate and difficult men in their lives.'

That was the pot calling the kettle black, Briony thought but did not say.

'This is Emma.' Nick strolled across the room. He pointed to a collage. 'Emma and her puppies. She was my black Labrador. Unfortunately I lost her last year.'

'Didn't you keep any of her puppies?'

'I was tempted, but the business got so hectic I had to devote all my time to work. Emma didn't mind, she was used to the routine. But to train energetic youngsters . . . no, I decided against it in the end. They all went to good homes, of course.'

Outside the snow was falling heavily, white fronds glazed across the glass of the windows. Briony found herself aching to bring up the subject of Samantha. But how could she? It was as if, by that single remark, Nick had kept the subject of Samantha Forbes dangling in the air. 'Stunning', wasn't it, he had described her? A pang of jealousy tore at her insides.

He was standing so close that she imagined she could hear the irregular passage of his breathing. His eyes looked dark and fathomless. Why wasn't Samantha Forbes Mrs Nicholas Lloyd, occupying this lovely country house, raising Labrador puppies and hordes of children? Why had he jilted such an enigmatic girl in preference for Lea, who seemed . . . Briony could only think of one word . . . shallow by comparison?

'It . . . it's a lovely room,' she said quickly, as much to put a stop to her train of thoughts as to fill in the silence.

'You like it? Surely it's too masculine a room for a woman?'

She shook her head. 'No, I don't very much like frilly houses. I prefer old, well-worn houses with all the characteristics of their owner.'

He chuckled. 'Oh, really? This sounds interesting.'

She found herself blushing. 'Well, I'm not sure I meant characteristics exactly . . . perhaps taste.'

'No, you said characteristics . . . you meant that. What in this room, for instance, is reflective of my personality?'

She arched a dainty eyebrow, her pale face warming under his gaze. A snowflake fell from her hair, melting on her cheek. 'You're sure you want to know?'

'I think I can take it.'

She gazed around. 'Well . . . this is a lovely room, a people room, an animal room. I can see dogs by the hearth in front of a blazing fire, a cat curled up there in the hollow of the windowsill. I can see the place full of life, newspapers rattling, a marrowbone being chewed on, some music drifting in from a radio somewhere. There's all the evidence of life . . . it's just . . . '

'You don't actually see it?'

Now Briony thought she probably had gone too far. It was none of her business. Aiming wild guesses was hardly fair, except that it was so like his character — so organised, every detail seen to, yet with the obvious ingredients missing. Notably a wife, children and sprawling tail-thumping creatures. The place was a snail without his shell.

'Anything else in that crystal ball of yours?'

'I don't actually know why I said all that,' she apologised nervously.

He laughed, white teeth glinting beneath full, amused lips. 'Well, I must say I'm a little surprised too. Pleasantly surprised. Do you know . . . Samantha . . . she didn't like this house at all? In fact, we were going to sell it. Buy something a little more in keeping with today's modern trends.'

'Oh.' It was all she could think of to say. Why sell a simply gorgeous house like this? And what had happened to make their plans fall through?

It was probably Lea. Yes, that was it . . . Briony gazed up at him, suddenly seeing the crooked smile on his face. He reached out a finger, guiding the tendrils of dark coppery hair away from her cheek and wrapping them gently back into the roundness of her neck. She felt entirely giddy. His touch lit up her body and her ears began that awful drumming, obliterating thought.

'Purely hypothetically, what would you do with a house like this? Dispose of it, go for something upmarket, or, as Lea has decided I ought to do, get in the professionals to give it a complete new fact-lift?'

So Lea did come here! And by the sound of it had no reservations about her future plans for the house. Briony slowly shook her head, thinking what a travesty it would be for anyone to lay a single finger on the place.

'Is that a no or a yes?' Nick's fingers now touched the nape of her neck, very slowly, teasing her skin, and the dark eyes drifted downwards to rest on the open fullness of her mouth, quivering now in anticipation.

'I . . . I don't believe in face-lifts,' she whispered, the sensual warmth of his skin sending off a salty aroma, making her feel languorous.

'Your kind of beauty would never require one,' he told her softly. 'You still look like the girl I knew a dozen years ago. Coming to terms with you being a professional lady has been just as difficult for me as I imagine it has for your father.'

Her eyes travelled to meet his. 'Father simply can't adjust yet; he will, in time . . .'

He drew her, very gently, into his arms. 'And what about you? Are you adjusting, here in Bagbourne or are you still set on independence and a career — and much later this . . . relationship of yours? I mean, how long is a relationship going to have to wait?'

Had she said that? Briony asked herself dizzily. The trouble was, at this moment he was driving her to distraction and she couldn't remember a thing she had said. But if she'd said it, she must have meant it! 'M-marriage, a . . . relationship, would only narrow my horizons,' she answered in a croaky voice, 'and — '

And then he kissed her.

She closed her eyes slowly, remembering with an exquisite pain the first time it happened. Her mouth was pulsing under the warmth of his lips. She wanted Nick with unrestrained desperation now. She knew exactly what trouble she was asking for, but the heaven of his kiss, his arms pressing her small body into his chest, was just too much to bear without accepting, utterly, that she adored every second. Her fingers travelled the firm line of his back to the nape of his neck. His skin felt rough on her smooth cheeks, his kiss became urgent, sending icy prisms of desire along the length of her spine. How much could she bear, how much could she take, loving him so much? It felt so right to be in his arms, and yet she knew it was disaster . . . she knew it . . . and yet she could do nothing to stop herself from falling in love with him.

When the phone rang, she almost jumped out of his arms.

His face was intense, even angry, as she pulled back, breathing unevenly, her eyes wide. 'It's the phone . . . ' she gasped breathlessly.

'Leave it.' He pulled her firmly back to him, lowering his head gently to her throat. The kiss burnt through her skin. Her body arched and she let out a small groan of delight.

The phone kept on ringing. Even if he could ignore it, she couldn't! But his hands made her forget to be sensible . . . stroking their way through her hair as his lips drifted down to the small valley of skin at the base of her throat. She closed her eyes, her thick lashes fanning her cheeks.

'Nick, you have to answer it.'

Reluctantly he drew up. 'Why?'

'It might be the surgery.'

'And it might not. Do you want to take the risk?'

She was bound to regret it if he was needed desperately and she was the cause of him not answering it. 'P-please answer the phone.'

The look he gave her was unbearable, as though he knew what she was thinking.

He muttered something inaudible

under his breath and, releasing her, walked out into the hall.

Briony felt torn between her emotions as she stood there shivering. Obviously he didn't find her alluring enough to resist the telephone, otherwise he would have silenced her simply by possessing her lips again — and surely he had known he had that power over her? She had made no attempt to stop him kissing her. To him, she was fresh, a distraction, enough of one to amuse him for a while. OK, she was a vet, she had accomplished that much, and she felt he respected her work, but he seemed to enjoy baiting her as a woman, leading her on to the point where she had no hope of recovering from the effect of those sensual lips.

Was this visit here made on purpose, to tease? Showing her the photograph, touching her the way he had, catapulting her into another world?

'It's Lea.' He was back in the room, pulling on his waxed jacket. 'She's had a road accident and has had to go in

259

to Theatre. Ben's out on his calls. The girls are holding the fort, but we'd better hurry.'

Of course it was Lea, Briony thought, realising that she was not only disappointed but angry too. Lea's antennae seemed to stretch to long distances even. No wonder Samantha Forbes had opted out. Lea was small and fragile-looking, but underneath she was as hard as nails. Briony wouldn't put it past her to work out that Nick was late because he'd called in at his house. And Lea's intuitive little mind would have worked overtime from there.

Nothing in his manner suggested that the pass he'd made had been anything but that — a pass. As outwardly calm as usual, he gathered the items he needed from the room. A wad of notes from a desk in the corner, his case and a spare coat from the back of the chesterfield. 'I'd make us a hot drink before we go . . . ' he said apologetically, his eyes finally alighting on her.

'We'll have one at the surgery,' she

answered, turning to the door. Falling in love was bad enough when you suddenly stopped deceiving yourself and admitted the truth, but falling in love and wearing your feelings on your face in front of someone like Nick was utterly stupid. Bravely she crossed the room, walked out into the hall and fixed her gaze on the coloured glass window of the oak door. She ignored the photograph on the table, knowing he was watching her. She wouldn't give him that much satisfaction.

They drove in silence. Nick seemed preoccupied, though the roads were dangerous and he had to focus his attention fully on them. She should think herself lucky, for how would that kiss have ended up? And how would she have felt afterwards, when the recriminations started? But she didn't feel lucky; she felt miserable.

When she reached the surgery, she hardly recognised it. A winter wonderland of pure white. And inside, it was true, bedlam was building up. Regretful that she had been so quick to damn Lea, she began helping out with the casualties.

She wished she could stop the incessant whirring of her mind and the pulse from beating thickly in her neck, always a bad sign. No man had ever made her feel the way Nick did when she was in his arms.

And, she supposed dimly, no man ever would again.

★   ★   ★

Briony stacked her parcels neatly by her feet and rummaged in her purse for change. Carols echoed throughout the shopping arcade, bouncing off the great Christmas tree, reverberating off glass windows.

She found some coins in her purse and threw them into the box provided for donations. Half a dozen young faces smiled up from behind sheet music. She picked up her parcels, the first of her Christmas shopping, trying to remember the things she knew she had forgotten.

The arcade was bustling. A ceiling above was studded with decorations sparkling and glistening like stars. Struggling with her purchases, Briony tried not to think of what Christmas would bring; her favourite time of year — normally.

'Stop it, Briony!' she told herself, squashing into her car with all her luggage. 'Don't think about it — or him. This is your day off, and you're going to enjoy it whether you like it or not!'

When she arrived home Beth was making the Christmas pudding, her brown hair swept back and icing stuck to her small nose. A jar of pickled onions lay opened in the middle of the laden table.

'Beer, brandy — or sherry?' she asked Briony as she fell in the door with her packages. 'Or all three?'

'All three,' laughed Briony, dumping the things, tearing off her coat with a deep sigh of relief. 'And pound coins, don't forget. We want our money's worth.'

'You'll be lucky!' Beth poured a concoction of liquids into her mix, making the air potent. 'I'm asking for donations for the cook this year. I think I'm worth a few tips.'

Briony leant across and sniffed. 'Phew! We'll all be drunk before we eat. Are you putting those in too?'

Beth giggled. 'I don't think anyone else would appreciate onions in their pud. Don says he's off them for life after seeing me guzzle so many.' She looked up at Briony. 'I'm going to start a few things for the dance next week. I thought I'd get cracking early.'

Briony pulled out a chair and, sitting down, she cupped her chin in her hands.

'For someone who's engaged to the most eligible bachelor in the county you look about as excited as that fridge over there. What's wrong?'

Should she confide in her sister-in-law? It would be a weight off her mind.

Ever since the day at Nick's house, she'd felt she had been going quietly crazy. But as she looked up at Beth, immensely happy with that alluring bump just appearing under her pinny, she felt she could not take the chance of upsetting her. 'I suppose I've been a little worried about Father, with Christmas coming up,' she said instead.

'You can stop worrying — I've got some good news for you. He's gradually changing his tune. Don and I had a surprise bouquet of flowers this morning from him. Look over there.'

Briony saw the gorgeous array of flowers, arranged in a vase on the window shelf. 'He sent you those? But why?'

Beth giggled. 'Silly! Can't you guess?' She stuck out her tummy as evidence.

Briony's small mouth quivered in delight. 'You mean . . . the baby!'

'His first grandchild — the first of a football team. Really, though, I can't see you and Nick having any less than half a dozen at least. You're both made for kids! You won't be able to get rid of your father then. He'll have them riding steeplechasers by the time they go to nursery school!'

It wasn't the thought of her father that made Briony gasp aloud, it was Beth's casual remark about children. Children! Her children — and Nick's! She had to say something now. She couldn't let Beth go on thinking things like this!

Briony was sitting rigid, trying to think of the best way to make 'Nick and I have no intention of getting married, let alone having children' sound less like an obituary, when the phone rang.

'See who it is, Bri, will you? My hands are all gooey.'

Slowly, turning the words over in her mind, Briony went to the phone.

'Briony? It's Nick.'

Her tummy churned immediately she heard his voice. Beth was staring at her from the table. 'It's Nick,' she mouthed, sure that the welt of colour in her cheeks was obvious.

'I've got a spot of bother. I'm on call over at the Bensons'. Do you remember treating their pony for laminitis?'

'Yes . . . what's wrong?'

'He's had another attack. Apparently he got out of his stable into the neighbouring farmer's field.'

'Oh, dear,' Briony sighed. 'I did try to stress the importance of keeping him in at all costs. The stable didn't look too secure. And I don't really think they accepted my diagnosis.'

'Well, they do now. Anyway, it's not that I'm too worried about. I've given him an injection of flunixin meglumine and he's back in his loosebox. But I want to hang around and take some blood tests. Unfortunately Joe Doyle has rung. He owns the stables I first took you to on our first day together. He's got a colic case. I suppose it's too much to ask for you to attend it? I mean, I know it's your day off . . . '

'Ben isn't available?'

'He is . . . but I'd prefer it if you went.'

267

She couldn't help but feel a stir of pleasure. Ridiculous, she knew. She was flattered — and touched — that he placed so much faith in her. Despite the fact she had planned an excursion to the hairdressers, she said immediately, 'All right, I'll go. I've a record of the address in my notebook, though I've a pretty good idea where it is.'

'I really do appreciate this.'

'Do you want me to come over to the Bensons' afterwards?' she asked on impulse, feeling responsible as they were originally her clients.

'No need. I'll hang on and make sure he's out of trouble, then I think I'll call it a day. Ben's taking over tonight for me.'

'See you Monday, then.'

'And thanks again, Briony.'

When she turned to face Beth she just hoped her pride wasn't showing on her face. He trusted her enough to leave an established client in her hands, one she knew to be cautious about having new vets to treat his stock — indeed, any other vet than Nick. She hoped he would phone the stables and make them aware of the arrangement.

'No peace for the wicked?' Beth remarked cryptically.

'No peace for a vet. But then you wouldn't want me hanging around getting under your feet in the kitchen all afternoon. Too many cooks and all that.' Briony tugged on her coat and picked up her case, trying to ignore the fact that she hadn't even managed to get her parcels upstairs into her bedroom, let alone help Beth with the cooking.

'What are you going to do when you're married and you have a ravenous male lunging at you and there's nothing on the table?'

Briony fled to the door. 'I promise I'll spend all day tomorrow slaving over a hot stove, though I don't guarantee the results, mind you,' she giggled, letting herself out into the cold afternoon air.

The snow, or at least the remnants of it, lay in dirty brown heaps spilling from the pavements into the gutters. Without the wipers on for once, she gazed up into a cold winter's sky, devoid of the greyness of past days but chillingly blue and empty of clouds.

Time had flown since her first visit here with Nick in October. Had she known how rapidly her life would change in just a few weeks she would never have believed it possible. Acknowledging her love for him was painful enough, but to have the whole of her home town actually believing they were to be married . . .

'Mrs Nicholas Lloyd . . . ' she said aloud. She said it again and again as she drove. And his house — that was even more disturbing. The place was so familiar, as though she knew every inch of it — *déjà vu*, perhaps? An everyday experience for some people. But nothing about Nick struck her as everyday. He was a contradiction in terms. She had tried many times to sort out how she really felt in the unravelled cohesion of her mind. He was a devil about women, that she knew. He worshipped his work and gave it the status he could not give to women in his life — faithfulness.

But did any of that matter now? If you loved someone like this, it transcended common sense and logic. Would there ever be a chance that he might take her seriously? Could she compete with women like Lea and Samantha?

Even if she could, what were the chances that, like the proverbial line of dominoes, she would have to fall down, eventually, in favour of another woman?

This was new territory to her, putting oneself in competition with other women. On a professional level she wouldn't think twice. She loved to compete; it was an integral part of her nature. But this . . . contest of the heart? She hadn't a clue how she would react if Lea were to bring the whole affair out into the open.

★　★　★

271

Joe Doyle's horses were fine thorough-breds. If he was having trouble with colic he would be worried. When Briony arrived at the stables he had, thank goodness, heard from Nick.

The job wasn't a particularly pleasant one. The horse she examined showed signs of a specific colic, an impaction of food material in the large intestine. A pain-killing drug had to be adminis-tered before she could carry out the examination of the rectum, feeling inside the horse's abdomen. Then, to stimulate gut movement while Joe kept watch, she administered liquid paraffin, a clearing agent and salt water through the rather uncomfortable means of a stomach tube.

By the time the procedure was over and the impaction successfully cleared she realised she wouldn't have had time to get over to the Bensons' anyway.

Joe shook her hand warmly as she left. He'd been a hard man, she had thought on that first day, to get to know, but now he was quite amenable, saying he hoped to see her again.

In an almost ebullient state of mind she decided she would return to the surgery before going home, to pick up a fresh batch of drugs for her depleted case. She didn't expect to be called out over the weekend, but by habit she kept her supplies topped up, avoiding the unnecessary journey back to surgery whenever possible.

Twilight fell as she arrived. She walked to the entrance, wondering if Lorraine or Anita would respond to her ring. She waited, case in hand, savouring the unearthly silence of the evening. More snow, she thought, was probably on the way.

'Briony . . . what are you doing here?' Lea stood there in the dazzling light, her mouth open in surprise.

'I might ask you the same,' Briony answered, stepping past her and walking inside. She knew Lea hadn't been on call, nor had there been surgery on Saturday afternoon. The door clicked behind her.

The young female vet looked very alluring. She wore a long cape with a large hood, her dark hair glistening under the lights, her fashion boots seductively covering those shapely calves. And by the look of her attention to detail, make-up and perfume skilfully applied, it was obvious that she wasn't at the surgery on business.

Lea shrugged. 'I might as well tell you. There isn't any point in trying to hide what I'm here for. I'm waiting for Nick. He's on his way back here from the Bensons' . . . he phoned me at my flat and suggested a drink.'

Briony felt the room swim. How could he do that? He had just told her he was finishing for the day. How could he be so two-faced? She had just spent the afternoon charging around on his behalf and foolishly imagining she was in love with him — and, if she was truthful, imagining she could change him.

'You look the worse for wear,' Lea continued, her violet eyes hard. 'I didn't think you were on call too.'

'I wasn't.' Briony bit her bottom lip in order to keep quiet. She wasn't going to let Lea guess how hurt she felt. She reminded herself that she had no need to be intimidated by Lea's tone or questioning. 'Nick asked me to help out as a favour.'

The skin over Lea's face seemed to tighten as she mulled over Briony's remark. 'Shouldn't you be asking why Nick's taking me out? Or does your little arrangement include you both going out with whomever you like?'

Briony's dismay turned rapidly to anger. Lea knew he was just using the engagement as a lever for his own purposes, and she wanted to flaunt the truth now! Well, she wasn't going to put her off quite as easily as Samantha Forbes. Briony suddenly realised she was fighting for something she hadn't known she wanted until this afternoon — or rather someone. She no longer felt sorry for Lea. Tilting up her chin, she returned the hostile stare.

'As far as chatting to the staff over a drink is concerned,' she answered coolly, 'it's Nick's right as an employer. I trust him to do just that.'

A look of incredulity creased Lea's face. 'Then you're a bigger fool than I thought you were. Don't you realise Nick's not looking for permanence in a relationship — at least, not your sort of permanence?'

Briony stood in shattered amazement. She opened her mouth, but she couldn't utter a syllable. The look on Lea's face made her flesh creep.

'Let me give you some advice, Briony. Steer clear of Nick; you're not in his league.'

Unconditional love? Was that what Lea meant? She was prepared to give herself to Nick no matter what the circumstances? Anger subsiding, Briony admitted to the full weight of the implication. Wasn't that what she herself had contemplated this afternoon? The façade of the engagement had given her yearnings legitimacy, but she had been deliberately blind.

And it had taken Lea to clear her vision.

She turned back to the door, pulled it open and walked quietly back out into the night.

10

The operation was lengthy.

Briony watched, fascinated by Nick's precision. His movements were swift, positive, instilling her with confidence. Once, she actually found herself holding her breath in anticipation.

He glanced up, his dark eyes enhanced, reflecting the intensity with which he carried out his work. 'How's he doing?'

She checked the anaesthetic machine, watching carefully for changes. Satisfied with what she saw, she nodded.

Nick went back to his work, recapping on the operation. 'Bruno's a strong lad. Though there's a genetic predisposition in puppies who grow rather rapidly, I think we've caught him just in time. An op like this is fairly straightforward if performed early enough.' Looking at her with a wry smile, he added, 'Shall we just go over the method again? What we've done is to remove this section of the ulna . . . '

Briony watched, briefly checking the St Bernard's respiration before swinging her attention back to Nick's fingers as they explored the site. She noticed that he was going a little slower than usual so that she could see quite clearly what he was doing. He had an extraordinary way of sensing just how much she was taking in, as though by repeating some points he knew her concentration had slipped. If it had slipped, it was simply because she was sidetracked by his large hands managing to do the most delicate of actions or by the way his eyes shot up every so often, locking into hers.

' . . . and we've placed a metal staple across the radial growth plate . . . thus.'

'What about the gap created in the ulna?' she asked as he began swabbing the area.

'It will heal. There's no need for support, because we've caught him in the first months of life.'

Briony watched quietly as he completed the final stages, intermittently talking through his movements. Finally he tied the last suture.

With the op coming to a close, despite the resolution she had made before coming into Theatre, her thoughts began to rove. How much opposition had Lea put up with regard to her assisting Nick with this op? It was an unusual one, and Lea wouldn't have wanted to miss it. Was that one of the reasons Nick had decided to take her out on Saturday night — to calm troubled waters? But she was looking on the optimistic side — that he had taken her out for no more than a casual chat. Even if he had it didn't excuse him telling her he had a free evening and insinuating that he was going home to enjoy it!

Withdrawing the needle, Nick frowned at her. 'You're quite clear on what we've done with this osteochondrosis? You would ask, wouldn't you, if I hadn't made myself clear?'

She nodded. 'I understand perfectly . . . you were very concise.'

He laid the syringe on the trolley and walked over to her as she began the clearing away. 'Is there something wrong?'

'No.' She averted her face, slipping off her mob-cap and allowing her thick hair to fall and cover the expression on her face.

'Is it Saturday? Are you upset I asked you to go to Joe Doyle's?'

She quelled the urge to tell him about the conversation she had had with Lea, biting her bottom lip. 'Of course not. I was happy to do the colic case.'

She buried her face even deeper into what she was doing. But suddenly her whole body seemed to crumble as Nick's fingers softly lifted the hair from her cheeks. He stared at her, his eyes flicking over the pale beauty of her face; the dark coppery cloud that haloed it, the freckles scattered like gold dust over the bridge of the small, straight nose and the Beaumont stare, ice-blue, as cold as Antarctica at this moment.

'Post-op nerves,' he chuckled, and to Briony's amazement turned to remove his gown and say nothing more on the subject.

Left alone, Briony finished her duties, trying to deal with her pent-up emotion. How could he drag her out on her day off just so that he could finish his calls in time to go out on a date with Lea? And the telephone call to her? He must have made it after he knew she was safely on her way to Joe's. He couldn't have any conscience at all!

How she had ever managed to keep quiet today she didn't know. Luckily there had been the St Bernard op to be done, and she was forced to disregard her personal feelings. Besides, what right had she to feel like this? The engagement was a pretence, and she was acting as though it were real. The word love hadn't featured once in their conversations, even hypothetically, but it had been the axis on which her world had been spinning for days on end.

Nick didn't owe her loyalty, although he did, to a certain extent, owe her the effort to keep up the charade at least until they agreed to dissolve it. How many people would have seen Nick and Lea together on Saturday night? Did he take her to meet friends, to a hotel, a restaurant?

'Stop it!' she hissed to herself through clenched teeth. 'You'll drive yourself mad, thinking like this!'

It was when Bruno had been removed to a specially prepared recovery cage and Nick settled himself down to wait for the first signs of recovery that Briony decided to do something about the matter. If she was going to get through the rest of the day she had better work off some of this destructive mental energy, or there were bound to be fireworks.

On impulse, at lunchtime she drove to the sports shop in Bagbourne, purchased a swimsuit, a luxury she had been promising herself for months, and chose a thick, soft bathing-towel as an afterthought.

She had three-quarters of an hour left for a swim. Instinct had driven her to the baths, and she was relying on it to douse the fire that was raging inside her. Changing into the summer-blue one-piece, with its fashionable high shape over her small hips, closely moulding the high round hills of her breasts, she felt quite confident about going into the water. True, it was six months since she had last swum, but she was a strong swimmer, and the energy that was bursting from her more than compensated for the time lapse.

She sliced the water. Diving from the edge with her head neatly tucked in, toes pointed, she slid under the surface, and hardly made a splash. As she came up for air in an almost deserted pool, several of the lifeguards gazed appreciatively in her direction.

Then she struck out. Crawl was her best style, and she ate the water, pacing her breathing rhythmically. It was hard at first — the shock of the cold, the different muscles she was using, cramping, then all at once blessedly relaxing, allowing her complete freedom of movement. For twenty minutes she forgot about Nick, the mental concentration of going through the pain barrier and out the other side being too enjoyable to allow him to creep back into her mind.

Arms shredding the water, long legs with a life of their own propelling her at such a speed, she barely noticed that she had an audience of burly males. Counting her twentieth lap, she was just beginning to enjoy herself. The blood was pumping so freely around her body that she felt she could have gone on forever. There was no effort in her strokes now; the water belonged to her. Nick was gone, banished; she was free as a fish in the ocean.

That was until the same instinct that drove her to liberation suddenly made her glance up to the great circular clock high above the pool. The fact that hordes of schoolchildren were arriving and a six-foot guard blowing his whistle frantically made her realise she had better stop.

'The pool's booked now for a school swim.' The lifeguard, bending down at the pool's edge, his brown body rippling muscularly, grinned at her. 'And I should think you could do with a break, couldn't you?'

Briony looked up, water dripping from her face, the long tails of her hair fanned out like a mermaid's. 'Oh . . . is that really the time?'

He laughed, his admiring gaze lingering on her. 'Whatever it is you wanted out of your system, I hope you've succeeded.'

Briony blushed to the roots of her hair as he took her arm and heaved her out of the water. 'Thanks. It was a great swim.'

'Great for us,' he joked, and, unwilling to let her arm go, cast his eyes over her long, slender body, the blue swimsuit revealing every inch in its clinging wetness.

The shower was heaven, hot and stimulating and far too good to leave so quickly. But she had to rush. Amid shouting, wailing adolescents she hurried to the car, with wet towel and swimsuit, bag, car keys . . . car keys? She didn't seem to have them in her bag or pockets.

Heart in mouth, she ran back to the locker. Which one was it? They were all in use now anyway. She glanced at her wristwatch — fifteen minutes late and she hadn't even got out of the swimming baths. Panic flooded her veins; she had an appointment for parvos in five minutes.

Rushing to the attendant, she asked about her keys. Since she couldn't remember the locker number, she was taken to the desk. At the desk she waited for what seemed an eternity. Finally someone opened the lost-property cupboard, and she sighed in relief, recognising her keys.

Driving to the surgery, she found

herself covered in a light perspiration. The sun had come to life during her swim and was dazzling through the windscreen. Cars flooded the roads as though it were summer. Diversions loomed everywhere, and she finally got stuck in a long queue, going hot and cold as she thought of her clients turning up to an empty consulting-room.

'What happened to you? We were worried!' Anita's expression made her writhe in guilt as she finally entered the surgery. 'And what's the matter with your hair . . . it's not raining, is it?'

A wet stream of water coiled off Briony's nose.

'Do you want a hairdrier?' Anita asked, frowning.

'No — later, perhaps. My clients, they'll be waiting!' Briony hurried to Reception, only to find it empty. Turning back with her heart pounding, she caught a glimpse of her reflection in one of the long mirrors. A wreck of a girl! Mac buttoned up on the wrong holes, hair straggling and legs bereft of tights.

'I saw to your parvo injections,' a deep voice said in her ear, 'ten minutes ago.' She swivelled on her heel to see Nick standing beside her, his face dark with an expression of shock. 'What's happened to you?'

Discreetly Anita slipped back into the office and closed the door.

'Thank you for doing my parvos.' The words seemed to get stuck in her throat. 'I . . . I took a swim.'

'You what?'

She walked cautiously into the hall, looking at him under her wet lashes. 'I thought a swim would be . . . a good idea.'

He looked taken aback. 'I'm sure it would have been . . . at the right time. Did you forget you had appointments?'

She jerked into awareness, her guilty feelings confusing her speech. 'I would have got back on time, but I lost my keys. I had to go back to the desk and they kept me waiting ages, and then I got stuck in all those diversions we came across the other day and I knew I'd be late, but I just couldn't — '

'Whoa! Slow down. Get your breath back.' Nick grinned, took her by the arm and steered her into her consulting-room. 'We have too many ears pricked around this place, as you've no doubt witnessed in the past. Sit down a moment.'

She sat, giving in to a deep sigh. She had completely panicked, but his reaction was totally unexpected. For some reason she'd thought he would be cross, or maybe she was just cross with herself for letting everyone down.

'Did the parvos go all right?' she asked, breathless.

'Splendidly.'

'And they didn't mind me not being here?'

He frowned, going to sit on a stool in the corner of the room. 'They did rather. The puppies asked me to tell you they were hopelessly disappointed you didn't show up.'

She looked at him searchingly,

realising this was a sample of his dry humour. 'No, really, I mean did it put anyone out, my not being here?'

He laughed, throwing back his head. 'You're not indispensable, you know. Good lord, you've worked all hours, filled in for staff on countless occasions, and you worry about being half an hour late back to work . . . once. What's the matter — do you think I'm going to eat you alive?'

Her blue eyes shone with relief as another pool of water emptied itself from the top of her head and lingered on her earlobe. 'No, I didn't think that, I just hate being late. I calculated too finely today — I don't know why — I'm usually the most punctual of people — '

'Briony, calm down, No damage has been done, thank goodness. To yourself, I mean. We were only worried about you because we know what an organised person you are, and Anita with her colourful imagination suggested a road accident. I was just about to ring Don.'

'But what if you hadn't been here?

What would have happened then? I was the only one officially on duty today.'

He shrugged. 'They would have waited or come back another day.'

She wiped away the moisture from her ear. 'Well, thank you . . . I don't know what else to say. And I don't really know why I went for a swim on the spur of the moment like that.'

'Did you enjoy it?'

'Yes.' She looked up at the object of her energies. 'Very much.'

'I might have joined you if you'd asked me,' he murmured with a rueful smile.

'I . . . I don't think that would have been a good idea. I wasn't very good company even to myself.'

He stood up, slowly walking behind her chair, his hands behind his back. He stopped. She dared not turn around.

'You're obviously upset, Briony . . . but it's more than being late, isn't it? Don't you think you ought to talk about whatever's worrying you?'

'I . . . I can't.'

'You mean you can't with me?'

She paused, cravenly afraid to admit the truth, but finally she did. 'I suppose so, yes.'

'Then it has to do with us?' He walked this way and that behind her, and still she didn't turn around.

'Yes.'

'Are you so unhappy working here?'

'No! I love working here. It's just . . . ' She couldn't say, It's just that I love you to the point of madness and seeing you every day is like having a knife go through my heart, knowing it will never work out. 'I feel too pressurised,' she said instead, 'not by the work, but by our . . . arrangement. I can't live a lie.'

He was silent for a moment, stopping dead behind her. 'You want to call the whole thing off?'

She gazed down into her lap. 'I do.'

He walked around her once more so that she could see the tips of his brogue shoes just in front of her. He said slowly, 'There's only one problem as far as I can see . . . as to calling it off. The engagement isn't exactly on . . . technically speaking, is it?'

She looked up at him. His face was serious. 'How do you mean?'

He indicated her fingers. 'You've no ring — everyone will have noticed that. We'll have to get you one before you can call off what isn't on.'

'But that isn't necessary, surely?'

'Necessary in so far as you must be seen to be wearing one, or it will look as if we've made this whole thing up, and then your father would probably never forgive you — or me. He's a perceptive man, as we both know very well. When he sees you next, the first thing he'll look for is that ring on your finger.'

She hadn't given a thought to this. But was he serious? Did he really feel that all the trouble of getting a ring was necessary? It just seemed as if it was making the matter more complicated. On the other hand, now she was aware of the problem it seemed an obvious mistake to have made, and one any fool would see through, let alone her father. She ought to have thought of it and perhaps found something at home to put on her finger. But she didn't have a home! She was living out of a suitcase! All her possessions were in store or with Greg still.

'The idea doesn't appeal to you?'

She shook her head. 'I just haven't considered it.'

'Then don't bother beginning now — I'll rustle up something. Have you any preference as to a stone?'

'Stone?' Briony felt her voice crack. This was the most peculiar conversation she had ever had in her whole life! 'No, of course not, but — '

The office door opened behind her and she was forced to swallow her words. Anita looked rather shocked. Had she overheard? 'Nick, phone for you.'

Feeling wet and a little chilly, Briony hovered, undecided as to what she should do as Nick walked past her and disappeared into the office. Continuing the discussion would mean waiting for the call to end, and several clients were, she could see, just making their way across the car park. She was relieved when Anita kindly whispered, 'Pop up to my room — the door's open. Hairdrier's on my dressing-table, make-up too. I'll keep the wolves at bay down here.'

Briony nodded gratefully and fled upstairs to Anita's flat. She discovered the hairdrier, arranged her hair, though it was in complete disarray after the swim, and she borrowed a pale lipstick and a spot of foundation from Anita's supplies. Taking off her mac and pressing her blouse and skirt into place, she wished she had thought to ask for the loan of a pair of tights. She must have left her own at the swimming baths. No matter — her legs were still fawn from summertime, her tan always keeping until January or February. Other than a coldness around her ankles and a heat of confusion in her heart, she looked respectable enough to begin the afternoon.

It was when she hurried downstairs and almost fell into Nick's arms at the bottom that she saw by the look on his face that there would be nothing respectable about the remainder of the day.

Gently supporting her by both arms, he said slowly, 'I'm sorry to have to break the news, but Don's just phoned to say Phoebe and Apollo were . . . attacked . . . by vandals this morning. As far as I can understand it, Phoebe at least is going to need medical attention.'

* * *

The barbed wire had been concealed, effectively, at the far end of the paddock, entwined over the fence and into the grass like some deadly trap.

'But who on earth would have done such a thing?' Beth asked as they all stood with the foal and her mare in the

297

field. Don had just finished untangling a separate sliver of wire from around Phoebe's hoof. A wound, about three inches in length on her point of shoulder, bled, but had been temporarily cleaned and stemmed by Nick.

Apollo stood quite still as Briony checked him, having been told by Don that in his mother's desperation to free herself from the wire she had sent him flying.

'There wasn't a darned thing I could do about it,' Don told them angrily, his face pale with distress. 'I just saw Phoebe rearing and I thought she might have been having a temper tantrum for some reason. I came running, but by the time I got down here it was too late. That damn stuff was camouflaged by the grass.'

Nick looked up from the wound on Phoebe's hind cannon. 'Not too deep here, but the shoulder cut looks nasty. Keep her still a few more minutes, Don, and we'll get her back into her loosebox. How's Apollo, Briony?'

Briony coaxed the frightened foal into standing still, running her hands over his loins and underneath along his ribs. 'Shocked more than anything. Grazes over the jugular groove, probably from the wire, but no penetration.' She felt a slight ruckling on his withers. 'And a long scratch here, but I don't think it'll need suturing.'

'They're sick, whoever they are,' groaned Beth, holding her riding coat around her and shivering with nerves. She wore slippers on her feet, suggesting that there had been panic stations at the outset.

Briony stood up, thankful she'd managed to find some spare jeans at work before she came. The sun, mellowing during the afternoon, was still warm, luckily, but all the same, Beth looked as though she could do with a hot drink to revive her.

Gently Briony put out her hand. 'Go back to the house and get some coffee on the go. There isn't anything else you can do here.'

'Yes, do that, Beth.' Nick straightened, a long strand of the wire in his hand. 'We'll disentangle all this stuff from the fence and grass and come back to the loosebox to do the suturing. A cup of coffee at the end of it would be most welcome.'

When she had gone, Nick raised an eyebrow at Don. 'Have you any idea who did it?'

Don nodded. 'I saw some lads throwing stones into the paddock last week. They didn't take too kindly to me telling them to push off.'

'You'll have to inform the police.'

'As soon as I've done this I'm going to. My fault really, for not keeping the pair of them in. But it was such a lovely afternoon I thought I'd see what Apollo's reaction would be to a glimpse of the outside world.'

'Let's get them back to the loosebox,' Nick suggested. 'We can come back and clear this afterwards.'

Phoebe consented to be led by a head-collar, her leg fortunately giving her no trouble as she walked. Apollo followed close behind, his neck still high in spite of his upset.

'You've got a good foal there,' Nick told Don as they arrived in the loosebox. 'He looks physically OK, but I'd like to give them both thorough examinations before we do the suturing.'

'Right. I'll coax Apollo into the adjoining stable and then if you don't need me I'll find myself a pair of wire cutters and go down and begin clearing up.'

Nick smiled, but caught Don briefly by the arm. 'I'd just see how Beth is first . . . she took it pretty badly, you know.'

Don groaned. 'Oh, God, yes! I'd forgotten for the moment . . .'

Briony watched Nick change Phoebe's head-collar after her brother had gone. She thought with admiration of how he had handled the situation, managing to calm her on the journey over, thoughtful of Beth, whereas her brother had almost forgotten he had a wife — and now, slowly and deliberately, he was changing Phoebe's head-collar for a bridle, smiling at her out of the corner of his eyes.

'How are you doing?' he asked quietly.

'Oh . . . OK. But I hate to think of people doing such ghastly things. What if Don hadn't seen it all happen?'

He nodded, but said quickly, 'Don't dwell on it — brooding never accomplished anything. Let's start, shall we? Go over her thoroughly, and then, if you'll kindly work your usual miracle in keeping her occupied, we'll prepare the area for suturing.'

Briony was glad he was there. If she'd had to deal with it, she would have felt far too emotionally involved and very angry. And that would have interfered with her concentration. Nick's objectivity made her realise, as he said, that there was no use dwelling on the possibilities of what might have happened.

'Like old times,' he muttered to himself after the examination, as he put local anaesthetic into the centre of the shoulder wound. 'This is where all our troubles began — with you, Phoebe, you old rascal.'

Briony held tightly to the bridle. Had he meant her to hear that remark?

'There. Now we'll wait awhile.' Nick straightened his long back, stretching, and Briony found her eyes glued to the expanse of body before her: broad chest, muscular underarms, a lean torso and long sturdy legs that, even in gumboots, made her insides jangle as she admired them.

She looked back at Phoebe. The minutes crawled by as the anaesthetic took effect. Finally Nick filled a syringe and, waiting for Briony to tempt Phoebe with some hay, he applied the needle to skin. Phoebe shook her head and Nick ducked, but Briony held on fast, keeping her still.

He grinned. 'All done. We'll give it plenty of time. Shall we see to Apollo while we're waiting, if he's not too skittish?'

In the adjoining stable Apollo stood nervously, obviously missing his mother. Briony felt an acute wave of sympathy run through her. He was the palest of grey-browns, long-backed and dazzlingly erect, and even in trauma he still held himself very bravely.

Nick slowly approached him, his strong arms gently going around him, persuading him into stillness. With a token toss of his head, the foal submitted to Briony's gentle examination.

'Apart from superficial bruising, I think he's going to be fine,' she pronounced eventually, knowing Nick was watching her. 'This cut doesn't require stitching, it's more like a graze, so I'll just clean it . . . he really is a sweet-natured little thing.'

After treatment, they watched for a while as the foal blinked his long lashes and ambled around. 'Let's get Phoebe done with,' Nick suggested beside her, 'and then we'll leave them in peace.'

Going through to the adjoining stable, they found Phoebe concentrating on her hay, one eye seeming to notice their arrival with an evil glint.

'Here goes,' Nick muttered, grinning.

Briony began her usual form of distraction, massaging the soft hair behind alert, rather dangerously pert ears.

'Just a little more antibiotic, then the suturing.' Nick worked quickly, and apart from one or two jerks making him stop briefly he finished the neat line of stitches, tying off and cutting the last one. 'Thanks . . . only an anti-tetanus left to do now.'

Strangely this was the injection Phoebe reacted to. She almost knocked the syringe out of his hand, but Briony hung on grimly to the bridle and he managed to finish the job as Phoebe swung round with an unearthly grinding of teeth.

Laughing, he weaved out of the way, grabbed Briony by the waist and chuckled, 'Let's make a move while we're still in one piece!'

She felt a physical thrill at his touch, reminding her, perversely, of what she had forgotten to remember over the last couple of hours. It all came rushing back like a horrible dream as they walked out into the crisply fresh afternoon air. She shivered, and he looked down at her, hugging her closer. 'Cold?'

'A little.' But coldness was not the reason for her shivering.

'Beth probably made that tea ages ago and decided to keep out of the way. Shall we go over to the house and put her mind at rest? Stress isn't going to do her little travelling companion any good.'

Briony looked up into the dark, distractingly handsome face. 'You think, even at this stage, the baby knows?'

'I do, as a matter of fact. I believe it's important to make him as comfortable as possible from the moment of conception. Comfortable physically in

306

the womb and comfortable emotionally.'

'Not everyone would agree with you these days.'

Nick shook his head. 'Maybe not. It's a very personal conviction, I suppose. But when I have a son I'm going to play him Chopin and Handel through that thin wall of skin, keep his mother free from all worries, talk to him, tell him what the outside world is like . . . '

A terrible pain struck just behind her ribs and she almost doubled up. Nick felt so strongly about an unborn child, and yet what of his attitude towards women? It didn't make sense. She just didn't understand him!

'You're shivering,' he said. 'Come along, let's get into the warmth.'

They walked to the house, his arm around her, and she was too weak, too hungry for his touch not to sink into its strength. But the weight of his words hung heavily in her mind. He seemed to know exactly what he wanted . . . his future was mapped out, precisely, characteristically. That beautiful house waited for someone. And her heart ached to think she would not be part of it.

★   ★   ★

Beth couldn't have said anything more crushing than, 'The dance on Saturday will be the perfect opportunity for you two to announce your engagement.'

They sat beside the roaring log fire in the drawing-room. Briony hoped they would think it was the heat that made her cheeks flame red. She drank her tea, her nose almost in the cup.

'Good idea,' Nick said as he sprawled across the sofa, his long legs taking up most of it.

'I'll just fill up the teapot.' Beth put down her teacup, giving Briony a withering stare for not looking more enthusiastic.

When she left the room Nick said, 'Perhaps that's a good idea of Beth's. You'll have the ring by then. It's probably an ideal time to make it officially known.'

With Lea looking on? Briony thought morbidly, knowing it was all just a hoax, for surely Nick would tell her. He set his cup down on the table, neatly into its saucer.

As casually as bidding someone good morning he added, 'Then a week of two later we'll say our differences are too great to resolve, and you can return the ring — if you want. I've no objection to you having it as a keepsake.'

Briony stared at him, not able to believe he could be so heartless. 'Keepsake of a broken engagement? How horrible!'

'It's not me who wants to break it.' He looked at her quite seriously, and she almost resorted to laughter. This was a joke!

'More tea, everyone?' Beth reappeared just as Briony was getting up. 'You're not going yet. Sit down for a minute,' Beth commanded. 'I'm going to make the most of having you both together in one place at one time.'

Briony desperately wondered how she could get off the subject of engagements. She had the ghastly suspicion that Beth was going to make a meal of it. She wished the telephone would ring or someone would knock at the door. But of course it didn't happen. It never did when you wanted it to.

Nick grinned at her, raising those thick bushy black eyebrows, bouncing the ball back into her court.

'I haven't finished making the list of who's bringing what yet,' Briony said, sitting down, hoping a change of topic to food affairs might distract Beth.

It didn't.

'I've seen to them all,' her sister-in-law answered with predictable efficiency. 'Left to you, Briony Beaumont, we'd have all ended up with cheese and Marmite sandwiches.'

Briony flushed, looking down into her cup. She hadn't helped at all, save to make a few cakes, and they had certainly evolved as no work of art.

Beth took another deep breath. 'Now, about the announcement . . . I thought we could organise some champagne — after all, it will be a special occasion.'

'Splendid,' Nick agreed, his eyes melting into Briony.

'But it's not — ' Briony began, hating him. Did he really get a kick out of this torture? 'It's not . . . '

'It's not for you to worry about,' Beth laughed. 'You can leave it all to Don and me.'

'No!' Briony jumped up, staring pleadingly at Nick. He had to say something or else Briony really would get champagne — and goodness knew what else.

'Super idea,' Nick said, uncurling his long body. The next thing she knew he had walked over and kissed her — hard! 'Stop worrying, darling,' he told her with mockery lifting his voice. 'Beth has everything in hand.'

Releasing her gently, he turned to Beth with a grin. 'I think I'd better go and give that husband of yours a hand before he works himself to a standstill.'

When he had gone, Briony was still standing rooted to the spot, her lower jaw sagging when Beth giggled, 'Anyone would think you were going to a funeral, Briony Beaumont! Just look at your face!'

11

Henry Dappledale yanked the collar of a small boy dressed in a turban and red chintz. 'You're tending that lamb, young 'un, not inspecting it for bugs. Leave it alone and come and stand by Mary.'

The boy dragged himself away from the stuffed sheep, blushing at the tiny girl who stood ramrod-stiff with a baby Jesus in her arms.

Briony smiled as she watched the children's tableau. Already the silver foil star had fallen down and the Wise Men had had fits of coughing and sneezing and looked more like sleepy-eyed gnomes.

'How much longer do we have to stand here, Mr Dappledale?' one of the Wise Men mumbled, scratching his turban.

'Till we've convinced everyone to

part with their money,' grunted the farmer unsympathetically.

'I'm tired. I want to go home,' a solitary voice protested.

Me too, Briony silently agreed. She was dreading the rest of the evening. She'd tried everything imaginable to get out of tonight, but no solution had presented itself over the last three days.

Clad in narrow jeans and a soft blue silk shirt decorated with silver strands, she wondered if anyone would miss her dressed like this. She could slip out easily amid the crowd. Then her heart sank as she caught Beth's eye across the buffet tables.

'Coming!' Briony mouthed, defeated.

She edged her way through the crowd. Festive balloons and a generous sprinkling of mistletoe hung down from the girders of the barn, under which a space had been cleared especially for the dancing. The group of musicians stopped playing briefly, as Henry tapped his fingers on the microphone and invited donations for Medlicott's new pigs.

Briony squeezed between the trestles and began offering paper plates and plastic knives and forks. Ben, serving his punch on the next table, shouted, 'That's how I like it, my women flocking to me. Come and have a glass!'

She laughed, shaking her head. 'And end up flat on my back?'

His eyebrows knitted wickedly. 'Damsels flat on their backs need resuscitating. You don't think I'm here without an ulterior motive do you?'

She smiled, watching him turn back to a young girl holding up a polystyrene mug. Behind her there waited other eager laughing faces and, beyond them, an ocean of revellers.

But no Nick.

The huge barn doors were pushed right back and a dazzling new moon shimmered in a silvery haze. Might he not turn up? He was on call tonight, and the chances of an emergency on a Saturday evening were pretty high . . .

'Enjoying yourself?'

The voice made her jump. She was staring right through Matthew Prior. He was dressed casually, wearing an open-necked shirt and no tie, but the navy blue corduroy trousers looked more fitting for a piano recital than a barn dance.

'Matthew! What are you doing here?'

'I'm waiting for you to come and dance with me.'

'But you never dance!'

'I came especially,' he said in a peeved voice as though he had gone to special lengths to turn up. 'Surely you're not going to refuse me one dance?'

She didn't want to dance with him; she had a feeling that he was going to cross-question her. But she didn't wish to appear impolite either. Reluctantly, she agreed.

Her instincts had been right. As soon as they were on the floor, Matthew drew her close, his hand wandering down her back adding pressure with his fingers. Her heart lurched in panic.

'You aren't really engaged to him, are you?' he asked her suddenly. 'I mean, I could tell by your face that day that you were as stunned as your father and I were.'

She looked up at him and his face was set. She recognised the spoilt, selfish Matthew she had glimpsed before.

'Don't go on with this act any longer, Briony, whatever hold he has over you. I know you're not happy — you couldn't be, not with his kind.'

'What do you mean — 'his kind'?'

'I mean he's a Lloyd. The family's no good — you know that.'

'Matthew, there isn't any point in our discussing this. I don't want to dance with you if you insist on — '

He gave her a little shake in his arms. 'Briony, the man's having an affair with another woman!'

She stiffened in his arms, her insides juddering. 'If you mean Lea, I know about that.'

'You do?' He looked as if he did not believe her. 'Do you also know he went through much the same pantomime with another girl a few years ago? Don't you realise you'll end up in the same boat as them?'

'How do you know all this?' Briony bit back weakly.

'I spoke to Lea. She's heartbroken, poor girl. I tried to coax her to come tonight, but she's too upset. It's a pity, because if I could get you to see what's perfectly obvious to everyone else — '

'You mean you tried to get Lea here to entice Nick away from me?'

'He wouldn't have needed much enticing.' Matthew's fingers were beginning to dig into her arms. 'Why do you put up with it?'

Tears pricked behind her eyelids. It was a very good question, and one she had asked herself many times. Why did she put up with it? Why was she here at all? Why did she allow Nick to cause her such emotional pain? And look at her now! Even though she knew

Matthew was right she still wanted to defend him. 'Please let me go, Matthew.'

'Not until I get some straight answers.'

'If you're looking for answers, why don't you try putting the questions to me?' The deep voice caused Matthew to release her and jerk around.

Nick stood behind him, his eyes burning darkly. He wore a blue corded open-necked shirt and blue jeans. His thick, glossy hair was carefully brushed back, the sight of a tiny scar on his forehead doing something quite indescribable to Briony's stomach.

'Well, do you want to continue this discussion here, or outside?' he asked Matthew in a calm, cold voice.

She saw Matthew stiffen, his mouth turning down at the corners. For a moment she wondered if he would have the courage of his convictions and tell Nick what he had told her — though, looking at Nick's face, she really wouldn't blame him if he didn't.

Matthew shot an angry glance back at her, then turned and shouldered his way through the crowd.

'He doesn't appear to be in a particularly talkative mood this evening,' Nick muttered, as he slipped his arms around her waist and drew her to him. 'At least, not with me. Was he bothering you?'

She tried to ignore the way her body was feeling as he held her. 'Not bothering me . . . just trying to talk some sense into me, I suppose.'

'Oh?' She felt the rumble of his voice through his chest vibrating into her own. 'And did he succeed?'

'He didn't tell me anything I didn't know already.' She suddenly felt exasperated. 'It doesn't really matter.'

'It matters very much, very much indeed.'

The music was beginning to get lively, and he bent to speak in her ear so that she could feel his warm breath on her neck. 'Let's get off the floor.' He gripped her hand, his strong brown fingers interlocking over hers. When they were in a quieter spot, he turned to hold both her hands, his eyes serious. 'Are you in love with him?'

Briony stood still, her heart beating so thunderously that she was almost deafened. Though the music blared in the background and people laughed and talked she felt as though she was in another world. She was too astonished to reply. Why on earth should he ask her that?

A deep frown creased his forehead as he insisted, 'I must know. You have to be quite honest with me.'

He really was serious! She half laughed. 'I've told you before, Nick, Matthew and I are only friends . . . '

'Just friends? Because back then when I had to break you up he didn't look like just a friend.'

She felt the blood rush to her face. 'If you really must know, Matthew was telling me he wanted to bring Lea here tonight because she was so distressed — '

'Is that all?'

'It's enough, isn't it? She's upset over you.'

Completely ignoring her remark, he asked her again, 'Then you aren't in love with him?'

'Of course I'm not in love with him!'

Suddenly she was in his arms, and the way he was kissing her made every other thought in her head disappear. His lips were so deliciously impatient that they melted her own open to a greedy response. His fingers reached up into her loose hair, splaying out the red coils, tightening with the sensual passion of his kiss. She felt the deep, rapid beating of his heart against her own, and when he gave her time to catch her breath she could only gaze up at him, thinking with a selfish pang of delight that no matter what anyone had said it was she who was in his arms tonight, and no one else!

'You didn't for a minute believe what he was telling you about Lea?' Nick whispered so softly that she barely heard him.

'You were listening!'

'No . . . not deliberately. But you were so engrossed in what he was telling you, I thought I was going to have to physically wrench you out of his arms.'

'Is it true, Nick?'

His lips touched her hairline, his breath like a summer breeze. 'Do you think I'd be here with you if it were?'

'But she told me herself you were meeting her that evening after I'd been to Joe Doyle's. She told me you rang her — '

His dark eyes narrowed as he interrupted her impatiently, 'I rang her because once and for all I wanted to clear the air. Anita told me she'd been giving you a hard time. What did you expect me to do? Let her get away with that sort of behaviour scot-free? What-ever made you think I was interested in her in a personal sense?'

'Everything!' she exclaimed hoarsely. 'From the moment I saw you out at Chez Françoise . . .'

'It was her birthday. She'd just broken up with her boyfriend. What else could I do?'

Briony closed her eyes briefly, thinking what a fool she had been to surmise so much. 'I . . . I didn't realise . . . ' Relief swept through her, almost as though she had taken a drug to cure some physical pain. Why had she decided to believe Lea — and Matthew? Why hadn't she listened to her own heart instead?

She opened her eyes to Nick's blank stare. 'Hey — what's the matter?' He held her gently away from him and with one brown finger wiped an escaping tear from her eyelid. 'Don't you know I've been teasing you unmercifully? Don't you know I've loved you from the very first minute I set eyes on you again? Do you really think I wanted you to work for me simply because Don owed me that miserable debt?'

She nodded, her mouth falling open. 'Yes . . . I did believe that.'

'Oh, my poor sweet!' He kissed her

again, uncaring about the people around them.

Feeling her cheeks glowing and giving him a little push, she asked, still not believing him, 'Do you mean you had . . . everything . . . planned from the beginning? Since . . . Phoebe?'

He grinned devilishly, the black pupils of his eyes widening. 'More or less. A few inspirational strategies came into play. Don't forget a man has got his pride to think about. I didn't know how you felt about Prior. And I knew you were a lady of . . . serious ambition. If I'd tried to sweep you off your feet all at once you might have turned me down. I had to make sure that wouldn't happen.'

Briony made a sharp intake of breath, her blue eyes incredulous. 'So when you told my father we were engaged . . . ?'

'Let's say I'd given the matter a fair share of thought in advance. I knew the chances were that we'd meet head-on. There was only one real solution . . . if I didn't want to lose you.'

She burst out with laughter. 'Nick! You are the most . . . ' and then her laughter died. That still didn't explain the photograph, the lovely young woman with chestnut hair. Even now, she just couldn't bring herself to say the name.

Incredibly and characteristically he said it for her in that slow, calm, reasonable voice. 'There's the small matter of Samantha too, isn't there?'

She nodded. 'You were right when you said I was jealous. And not only of Lea. When I saw that photograph of . . . of Samantha . . . '

'Samantha and Luke. Didn't you recognise him?'

She shook her head, suddenly remembering that at first she had thought the man with Samantha had been Nick. 'But what has Luke got to do with her?'

'Quite a bit. She's his wife.'

'Oh, Nick . . . ' her breath stung in her throat ' . . . I didn't realise. I'm sorry!'

'Don't be. I know now that what I felt for her was nothing in comparison to the way I feel about you. We'd have made a grave mistake if we'd married. But she was charming, intelligent, she had ambition. I was fascinated for a while . . . '

Briony looked up at him, remembering the over-powering drive of her own ambition. It was there still, but love had overtaken all. She wanted to share the rest of her life and her future with him . . . she could only hope he felt the same too. 'What went wrong?' she asked hesitantly.

'Luke came over from Canada. He's a highly successful businessman, as charming and ambitious as Samantha herself. They hit it off at once. As simple as that.'

She suddenly ached for him, remembering the smiling, self-assured Luke in the photograph. Even as a girl she had considered Luke dashing, rather film-starlike.

'It must have been a terrible shock

for you,' she said softly, wondering achingly if he still felt anything for Samantha.

Dispelling her doubts, a smile transformed his face. 'I believe it was a narrow escape. I didn't want a woman to change my life, I wanted one to share it. And Samantha wouldn't have settled for being a vet's wife. Not many women do.'

'What do you want of the woman in your life?' she asked, her cheeks going the colour of strawberries.

'I want her to love me as I am.'

'Rambling old house and all?'

He laughed, throwing back his head. 'Yes, rambling old house, dogs, infants . . . and all.'

Briony put up her hand and felt the light stubble on his chin, so dear to her, because it reflected that he had hardly had time to change tonight . . . and it must have been a mad dash to get away from whatever animal he was treating. She traced her finger along the thin scar stretching across the line of his jaw, drew it slowly over his lips. And she felt her whole body tremble in joy. 'I love you, Nick.'

When he kissed her again, deeply and searchingly, she knew her love was returned, more than she had ever dreamt was possible. 'I can't believe this is happening,' she murmured, her eyes wide, her skin flushing creamily.

'If you love me, you'll marry me. I'm afraid I won't settle for anything less.'

'I wouldn't want anything less. I never have.'

'Then you fooled me, Miss Beaumont. I wasn't at all sure you were the marrying type.'

'What type did you imagine I was?'

He grinned. 'The career girl, the dedicated-to-her-vocation category . . . '

'I am,' she laughed gently, 'but I think I can fit you in between times.'

His strong arms gave her a playful hug. 'You've got a nerve. Come on — before you start changing your mind. I'd like you to meet someone.'

She found herself walking on air. She

was far too aware of the presence of his body beside her to care whom she was going to meet! Her hunger for him just seemed to drown the last remnant of sensible thought. Beth's champagne would never match this euphoria inside.

'He's over there, with your brother . . .'

She felt herself blink and sudden recognition take place through the mists of her happiness. Could it be? It surely couldn't! Nick gave her a little push. 'Come on, no cold feet now!'

Don was lost in conversation with a man she had last seen in a photograph . . . greyer, and a little less upright, but still the same man who stood proudly with his two teenage sons. Sebastian Lloyd stretched out his hand and she found herself taking it. 'Briony . . . it's been rather a long time, hasn't it? How many years?' His smile was kind, reassuring, like his son's.

'I . . . I'm afraid it's far too many,' she stammered, smiling back nervously.

'Nick came to tell me he was thinking

of getting married. I must admit I was rather surprised at first. But now the reason for his change of heart is obvious — congratulations, my dear. I hope we can forget all the unpleasantness of the past. I'd even hoped your father might be here and I might be able to talk to him.'

Nick pulled her gently against his broad chest. Seeing her disappointment at the older man's words, he said reassuringly, 'It won't be long. One day he'll come to see reason.'

A part of her agreed with him. She knew it would take time. But if Nick's father could forget the past, then surely her own could.

Distractingly the music seemed to blare, and she felt Nick's impatience to guide her to one side. Vaguely she sensed Sebastian and her brother moving off, absorbed in conversation. Nick's hand came up to her chin to bring her mouth gently to his. 'I love you, my darling, you funny girl.' His mouth teased as he drew her to him.

She lingered in the warmth of his arms, not caring who saw. Her life had changed irrevocably tonight, and she was going to make the most of it. She didn't care what happened tomorrow, at least not until she woke up and asked herself if this had really happened.

'I almost forgot! I've got something for you, something I promised,' he said, breaking away from her arms and making her jump. Delving into his jeans pocket, he carefully brought out a small box. She gasped as he flipped it open to reveal a glittering band of gold bearing a cluster of sea-blue stones.

'I hope the size is right. Beth came with me to try it on. Both of you have slim fingers.'

'Beth? You mean . . . she knew about all this?'

He laughed, his dark eyes mischievous, and for a moment Briony was visited with a horrible suspicion that this all might be some terrible joke. But he added, 'Don and Beth have known from the very first how I felt about you.'

'You told them?'

'I didn't want them thinking their future brother-in-law was a scoundrel.'

She felt an exquisite thrill as he slipped the ring on her finger, and it fitted perfectly. 'It's beautiful, Nick!'

'I was planning to do this outside in the moonlight without any spectators — make at least one memory so romantic you'd never forget it. A vet's wife has some pretty unromantic situations to deal with!'

She looked up at him, thinking how every single memory she had of him would never be forgotten. He was the most romantic, sexiest, stubbornest, most surprising man in the whole world!

'Blue is the colour of my true love's eyes . . . ' He kissed her softly. His eyes were calm as a mirror . . . just looking into them made her ache with desire. Suddenly she wanted to be alone with him, completely alone.

'Yes, let's go outside,' she said softly.

A wry smile touched Nick's lips as he picked up a rug from a bale of straw and folded it around her. A little shiver ran down her spine as he guided her through the barn doors and out into the crisp, moonlit evening. The silence lay around them like a tranquil sea.

They leant against rough wooden fencing, and he coiled her into his arms. His kisses caused her restless and quivering body to ignite, and a small moan of joy left her lips as she felt his body hard and firm against hers.

'I couldn't find a box large enough,' he drawled slowly, grinning at her, 'to wrap your wedding present. Otherwise you should have had that too tonight.'

'Tease!' she giggled in mock-surprise, thinking no more could be added to her already overflowing cup of joy. 'I don't believe anything you say any more!'

Pushing back her tumbling hair with both hands, he slid his fingers around her neck and with his thumbs tilted up her chin to the moon, staring at her in its light. 'I'm telling you the truth. Aren't you in the least little bit curious?'

She laughed, her curiosity, as ever, far too rampant. She held her breath, trying to see into those dark pools which had caused so many conflicting emotions to stir in her body. 'I'm hugely curious . . . you know I am! But I'm beginning to think you can read every thought in my head.'

'Not every one . . . but most.' Nick grinned, his white teeth making her heart see-saw, exposed like pearls in the moonlight. 'Kiss me again and then I'll tell you.'

Briony encircled his neck with her arms and he pulled the blanket around them. Standing very slowly on tiptoe, she began the journey towards his lips . . .

'Mr Lloyd!' A shout rang out across the night. She froze in his arms, as though she were waking from sleep. Had she been dreaming? Was this a wonderful, never-to-be repeated dream?

'Over here!' Nick shouted, cursing under his breath as he released her.

A young lad, no more than sixteen, rushed towards them. 'Me dad's got a cow that's gone down and we just can't get her up.'

'Where?'

'Down the road from here, not very far. Can you come?'

Nick glanced back at Briony, his face familiarly intense. 'Hurry up and go,' she said, with her heart racing. She could wait. She could wait forever now.

'I'll be with you in a few minutes,' he called to the boy and then he came back to her and took her in his arms. 'I am on call . . . '

'You'll always be on call, my darling. Animals are our life . . . and I hope it won't ever be any different.'

He grinned at her, kissing her softly. 'Talking of animals, Don has sold Phoebe.'

She stared at him, her heart sinking. 'No!'

'Yes, my love. She's to go as a wedding gift ... to a young woman with hair the colour of autumn forests.'

'Nick ... you haven't! Have you?'

'Could we ever see her sold to someone else?'

Her lips shuddering, she wound her fingers through his hair. 'How many more surprises have you got tucked up your sleeve, Nicholas Lloyd?'

'Just this one ... ' And then he kissed her.

'You'd better hurry, my darling,' she whispered gratefully, her eyes alight with love.

'I must be mad, leaving you.'

'All vets are probably a little mad,' she laughed, his fingers slipping from her.

His shadow melted into the darkness and she listened for the sound of his voice in the distance, her heart responding with its own silent call.

A star, an exceedingly bright one, spun its light down from the sky, momentarily blinding her, reflecting its magic in the cluster of stones on her finger.

He would be back.

And this time she would be waiting for him.

THE END